MW01482783

Romance 101

Forty-two
Light, Sweet, Delicious, G-rated
Short Stories

Sweet ~
Jan Bono

Jan Bono

Sandridge Publications
www.JanBonoBooks.com

Copyright © 2012 by Jan Bono

All rights reserved. No part of the contents of this book may be reproduced, transmitted, or performed in any form, by any means, including recording or by any information storage and retrieval system, except for brief quotations embodied in critical articles or reviews, without written permission from the author.

First Printing, Fall 2012

Printed in the United States of America
Gorham Printing, Centralia, WA 98531

Sandridge Publications
P.O. Box 278
Long Beach, WA   98631

http://www.JanBonoBooks.com

ISBN: 978-0-9838066-7-7

DEDICATION

To all the hopeful romantics
who unfailing see the relationship potential
in every chance encounter.

INTRODUCTION

Boy meets girl.

Yes, it's an age-old story, but every single one of those stories had its own special beginning. The planets aligned at precisely the right instant for the paths of two specific and potentially compatible people to cross.

But how? Where? When? Why? And what were the circumstances of their first "hello?"

The odds may have been stacked high against them, but nevertheless, they met. Where they go from here is anybody's guess, but the opportunity for a loving and respectful relationship now certainly exists.

Boy meets girl.

I've always been intrigued by the magic that made a chance encounter possible. With millions of single people wandering about the world, is it luck or destiny that brings a new couple together?

I hope you enjoy these 42 stories, and I hope you are inspired to keep your eyes and heart open to romance.

Yours truly,

Jan Bono

CONTENTS

A Puppy in Her Pocket

Carl took a window seat in the small diner and unfolded his newspaper. It wasn't that he was anti-social, he was just shy, and new in town.

The waitress came promptly with a glass of water and his menu. Carl nodded his appreciation, and took the menu without looking directly at her. He briefly scanned the daily specials, and was thoroughly engrossed in the newspaper when she returned a few minutes later.

"I'll have the meatloaf special," he said, not taking his eyes off what he was reading.

"And what kind of dressing on your salad?"

Carl detected a little sniffle at the end of her question. He looked up, and into the most beautiful brown eyes, with the reddest rims, he had ever seen.

"Ranch."

"Anything besides water to drink?" She sniffed again.

Carl couldn't stand it. "Miss?" He peered at her nametag. "Donna? Are you all right?"

Donna shook her head, and the tears she'd been holding back began to flow down her cheeks.

"What can I do to help?" asked Carl.

"My dog had puppies." All in a rush, Donna managed to choke out, "and they're six weeks old now and my landlord says I can only have one dog in my apartment and the puppies have to be gone by next Monday or he'll take them to the pound."

"What kind of puppies?" asked Carl.

Donna reached down into her apron pocket and retrieved a small ball of black curly fur. "The best I can figure is that they're cocka-pomma-peeka-poo."

Carl burst out laughing. Even Donna managed a small smile.

"You see?" she offered the puppy to him. "He has a cocker spaniel head, a plumy Pomeranian tail, stubby little Pekinese legs, and the curls on his ears and rear-end are definitely poodle."

Carl took the tiny dog from her and held it gently in one hand. "A cocka…pomma…peeka…poo… Well, what do you know?"

The puppy licked his fingers. "He likes you," said Donna.

"Do you think he'd still like me if he knew I worked for the Health Department?" He handed her his new business card.

"Oh no!" Donna gasped and put her hand over her mouth. "Please don't report me—Carl," she pleaded, reading his name off the card. "I don't want to get fired."

"Don't worry," said Carl, stroking the top of the puppy's head. "I'm not at work right now, and I'm sure he won't be here when I return tomorrow with my official 'on-duty' clipboard."

"I promise," said Donna. "You'll never see him in here again!" She reached out to take the puppy back, but Carl pulled him closer.

"Does he have a name?"

"I call him Brutus."

"Brutus?" Carl laughed again.

"But you can call him anything you want," said Donna hastily.

"Whoa now!" said Carl. "I never said I wanted a dog."

"Do you?" Donna looked at him with her big brown eyes and Carl's heart began to beat wildly in his chest.

"Well, now that you mention it, maybe I do." He paused for a moment, thinking it over. "I just moved here and my house does seem kind of empty… And the house has a big backyard and plenty of room for a dog to run… Especially a dog this size." He smiled.

Donna smiled back. "Then you'll take him?"

"On one condition."

"Anything!" said Donna.

"How many puppies do you have left?"

Donna lowered her eyes and sighed. "If you take Brutus, I'll have three more to find homes for."

Carl smiled. "Then my condition is that I'll take Brutus if you'll let me take all four of the pups—just until you find good homes for the other three."

Donna's grin stretched from ear to ear. "Oh!" she exclaimed, bouncing up and down in excitement. "I could just kiss you!" Then, realizing what she'd said, she blushed deeply. "Well, you know what I mean."

"Yes," Carl replied, graciously letting her off the hook, "I know exactly what you mean."

He looked down at Brutus, who was curled into a small ball and apparently asleep in his hand. "Donna?" he asked cautiously, "Are the other three puppies in the kitchen?"

"Good heavens no!" laughed Donna, shaking her head. "They're still at home. I'll take my break right away and go get them."

"Uh… Do you mind if I get my dinner first?"

"Oh my goodness!" exclaimed Donna. "I forgot all about it!"

"That's okay," said Carl, "but I am getting pretty hungry."

Donna nodded. "And you'll need to eat to keep up your strength if you're going to be chasing four puppies around that big backyard."

"Yes," agreed Carl, meeting her eyes. "And might you be available to come help me with that?"

"I might be," said Donna happily, turning toward the kitchen. "I just might be."

Love is in the Air

All morning her co-workers had been good-naturedly referring to Marie's birthday as "doing the speed limit." Personally, she thought it was more like "hitting the big speed bump." Fifty-five! How in the world had that happened?

"I got you something that will definitely cheer you up," said her best friend Alice, handing her an envelope during their lunch break.

"I thought we agreed not to exchange gifts any more."

"Oh, pshaw," replied Alice with a grin. "I couldn't help myself. Not when I knew it was something you really wanted."

Warily, Marie opened the envelope. "Oh my!" she exclaimed, reading the gift certificate. "Oh my!" Her eyes misted over. "Alice... How did you know?"

"You shouldn't leave lists like that out on your desk," replied Alice.

"You read my bucket list?!"

"It's not like I was snooping or anything. It was just lying there where anyone could read it. That's how I knew this was a gift you wouldn't refuse or exchange!"

Marie sat looking at the paper in her hands. "Scenic Helicopter Tours," she read aloud, shaking her head. "You're right, Alice. This is something I'm definitely going to enjoy.

Saturday dawned bright and sunny. Marie drove to the airport humming along with the radio. *Today's the day,* she thought. *Today I'm going up, up and away!*

"We don't take singles on any of our tours," the woman in the charter office told her. "You'll have to wait until we have another passenger or two."

Marie nodded. "I don't mind waiting," she replied. She stepped outside to take a few pictures of the small, bright yellow whirlybird parked nearby. It wasn't long before another car pulled into the lot. A man and woman got out and went into the office.

The man soon emerged and approached Marie. "I'm James," he said, extending his hand. "Would you mind if I shared a tour flight with you?"

Marie shook his hand. "Not at all," she replied. "Is your wife coming with us?"

"My wife?" James laughed. "I'm not married. That's my sister, Karla. It was her idea for me to go flying today." He paused. "I've never been in a helicopter before, and she thought it would be a good birthday present."

"What an amazing coincidence," said Marie. "This is my birthday gift from a girlfriend at work, and I've never been in a helicopter either."

James laughed again. Marie liked the sound of his laugh and the way his eyes crinkled at the corners when he smiled. "Seems we have a lot in common." He tilted his head and looked closer at her. "Don't tell me it's on your bucket list, too?"

"Of course it is!" Marie replied, laughing. "And today, thanks to you, I get to cross it off that list."

"Thanks to me?"

"They won't do a scenic tour with just one

passenger."

"Then I guess I have you to thank as well." James took her by the elbow and turned her toward the office. "Now let's get this show on the road."

Soon they were boarding the chopper and adjusting their headphones so they could talk to the pilot and each other during their flight. Marie felt little butterflies dancing in her stomach, and stole a look over at James, who was fidgeting with his microphone.

He caught her looking at him and smiled sheepishly. "I'm a little nervous," he admitted. "How about you?"

Marie smiled. "I'm just fine," she fibbed.

As the pilot explained to them what they were going to see on the tour, Marie suddenly noticed the ground getting farther away. "Oh!" she gasped, "we're already airborne! That was so... smooth!" She was thrilled and a little scared at the same time. A shudder ran through her.

James reached over and took her hand. "Do you mind?"

"Mind?"

"Is it all right if I hold your hand? It would make me feel a lot safer."

Marie giggled nervously. "You know we're not alone up here, right?"

"Right," said James, squeezing her hand. "I'm well aware that we have a chaperone in the front seat."

"Have I mentioned," interrupted the pilot, "that we also do weddings aloft?"

"Whoa there," said Marie, giggling again. "Why don't we all just sing 'Happy Birthday' and hold off on the wedding march?"

"I agree," added James, nodding slowly and looking

deep into her eyes. "And perhaps I can sing "On the Wings of Love" some other time.

Marie felt her cheeks growing warm. She continued to gaze out at the beautiful landscape below. A prolonged silence began to stretch between them.

"Have I also mentioned," the pilot interjected, "that a helicopter doesn't have wings?"

Marie looked over at James. Wings or no wings, her heart was soaring. She began to wonder what else she'd soon be crossing off her bucket list.

Love Birds

Abigail loved the fresh-baked smells of donuts and maple bars and other pastries. That was one of the reasons she made the extra stop at the bakery every morning to pick up a cup of coffee. She just liked to breathe in the delicious aromas.

Today, though, the line seemed to be moving at a snail's pace, and she gazed longing into the display cases, wondering how many extra laps at the pool she'd have to swim if she indulged.

As the line inched along, she passed a full rack of "day old" goodies at significantly reduced prices. The top shelf sported the fancier items, the second held an assortment of specialty breads, and the bottom shelf said simply "Bird Bread." Abigail laughed, and on impulse, took a bag from the bottom shelf.

"What kind of birds are you feeding?" asked the man behind her. She turned and was immediately impressed by his dark-chocolate eyes and engaging smile.

"I hadn't quite gotten that far," Abigail said a little sheepishly.

"You mean you don't usually feed any particular birds?"

"I mean I've never fed any birds. I just thought it might be a nice thing to do." She laughed. "I guess I better give the whole idea some more thought."

"Well, if you want suggestions, there are plenty of ducks on the lake this time of year. And of course there are always seagulls looking for a handout if you want to take the short drive over to the beach."

Abigail smiled. "Thanks for the suggestions." She might have said more, but it was finally her turn to pay. She would feel silly standing there, waiting for him to check out, so she gave him a little wave and went on to work.

From time to time throughout her day, Abigail mentally kicked herself. *What's the matter with me?* she wondered. *Why can't I ever think of something clever and witty and charming to say?*

Shortly after 5 o'clock, Abigail got into her car and stared at the bag of "Bird Bread" sitting on the passenger seat.

No time like the present, she thought, and drove the 20 minutes to the beach. She pulled over on the side of the beach approach road and parked behind a small dark blue car. The person sitting in the car ahead of her was throwing an occasional French fry out the window, and had attracted quite a gathering of gulls.

Stepping out of the car, Abigail opened the bag of bread and tossed a handful of slices toward them. She was instantly mobbed, the birds squawking and squealing and beating the air with their wings as they fought for possession. Abigail turned and ran back to the safety of her car. She sat there a moment, feeling rather shaken up by the experience.

The driver of the little blue car stepped out of his vehicle and walked back toward her, smiling. *What are the odds on this?* thought Abigail. The man approaching her was the man from the bakery, grinning from ear to ear.

Abigail rolled down her window. "It's really not all

that funny," she said.

"I wasn't laughing at you," the man began. He looked at his feet. "I was smiling like that because I was hoping I'd get to see you again."

"Well," said Abigail, once again at a loss for words, "here I am."

"So I see." He paused, then put out his hand. "My name's David, by the way."

"Abigail." She stuck her hand out the window to shake his. After yet another moment of rather awkward silence, she spoke again. "I guess I have a little to learn about feeding the birds."

"I bet you thought you were in an Alfred Hitchcock movie for a minute, didn't you?" He smiled, and then his expression turned more serious. "I just happen to give bird-feeding lessons," he began. "Are you interested?"

Abigail laughed and tentatively got back out of her car. She handed him the bread sack. "Sure, David," she said, "show me how it's done."

He reached into the bag and tore off a small piece of one slice. "Just a little at a time works best," he said. "That way they don't go so berserk fighting over a whole bunch at once."

Abigail tilted her head and looked at him. "That's a good idea," she said.

David smiled as he threw the last of the bread crusts toward the birds. "I have a lot of good ideas."

"Oh yeah?" said Abigail, teasingly. "Like what?"

"Like maybe meeting me for coffee at the bakery tomorrow morning?"

Abigail pondered his invitation for a moment. "You're wrong," she finally said. "That's not just a 'good' idea, that's a great one!

Chapel of Love

Jenny stood behind the chapel's reception counter and wondered how her aunt had talked her into helping out this weekend. It wasn't like Jenny had anything else to do, and she could always use the money, but working here only reminded her that she had yet to meet the man of her dreams.

Her daydreaming was interrupted by the front door chime: "Here comes the bride." The chime was kind of hokey, but the patrons seemed to enjoy it.

"Hello!" Jenny beamed at the young man who entered the lobby. "Welcome to the Chapel of Happy Holy Matrimony. How may I help you?"

The man looked around uncomfortably. "Well, you see, the bride's plane was delayed a couple hours, so I need to reschedule the chapel, and..." He approached the display case under the counter in front of Jenny and peered inside. "And I want to find something that will cheer her up. When she called to inform us she'd be late, I could tell she was pretty upset."

Jenny nodded sympathetically. "We're all at the mercy of the airlines, I'm afraid." She opened the wedding registration book next to the cash register. "So who was the ceremony for, what time was it supposed to take place, and when would you like to reschedule it?"

"Benson and Wilcox," he replied. Abruptly, he

extended his hand. "I'm Matthew Wilcox, by the way. And the ceremony was supposed to be at three. We'll need to make it anytime after six. Whenever there's an opening."

Of course, thought Jenny. *He's the groom. No wonder he's all flustered.* "Jenny Saunders." She shook his hand. "Pleased to meet you."

Jenny quickly erased the original chapel reservation and scanned the rest of the entries. "You're in luck," she said. "There's one service set for 6 p.m., then the rest of evening is entirely open."

Matthew hesitated, then took out his cell phone and quickly punched in a number. "Mom? I'm at the chapel. You think Cheryl will be able to pull herself together by seven?" He nodded while he listened, then said good-bye and flipped the phone shut.

"Seven o'clock it is," he said to Jenny. He looked into the display case again. "And I'd like a pair of those black and white embroidered Bride and Groom baseball caps. Those ought to make her eyes light up again."

Jenny rang up the sale and handed him the caps and receipt. "Will there be anything else?"

Matthew paused and then quietly asked, "Will you still be here at seven?"

What was he doing flirting with her when he was about to get married!? She felt like giving him a piece of her mind, but just shook her head. "I'm temporarily filling in for my aunt. She runs the counter and Uncle Ray performs the ceremonies. I'm sure Aunt Lydia will be able to help you with anything you need this evening."

Matthew nodded and left, the door chimes ringing again as he departed.

Good riddance, thought Jenny.

But when the time came for her aunt and uncle to

return, only Uncle Ray appeared. "I'm sorry, Jenny," he began. "But Lydia isn't feeling well. She told me to ask you if you'd be so kind as to stay on another couple hours."

"Of course, no problem Uncle Ray." Jenny smiled understandingly, but inside she wondered how she would deal with the flirting groom.

At quarter to seven, in came Matthew, escorting a beautiful woman in an equally beautiful wedding gown. They were accompanied by an entourage of 10 or 12 happily chatting wedding guests.

"You can all go right on down the hall," said Jenny, not meeting Matthew's eyes. "The second door on the left."

A few minutes later, Matthew reappeared. "Jenny?" He looked at his watch. "We seem to have a little problem."

Jenny waited for him to continue.

"Bryan isn't here yet, and he's not answering his cell phone."

"Is Bryan the best man?" asked Jenny.

"Is Bryan the best man?" echoed Matthew. "No, Bryan is the groom, and I don't think my sister Cheryl can take many more delays today."

The front door suddenly chimed, and a man Jenny assumed was Bryan came dashing into the lobby. "Matthew! I couldn't find a cab so I ran the whole way from the hotel!" He turned to Jenny and smiled. "You must be Matt's wedding date! He's told me so much about you."

Matthew blushed. "Jenny, would you like to come to my sister's wedding? Then maybe afterward, we could go have a cup of coffee?"

Jenny walked over to the door and hung a 'closed' sign in the window. "Matthew, your sister's very lucky to have a brother like you, and I'd be delighted to be your date tonight."

Snowcapped Lesson in Love

Marc double-checked the list on his clipboard. Raquel Livingston was late for her first snowboarding lesson. He looked at his watch and wondered if someone in the office had written her name in the wrong time slot.

He glanced at his watch again and scratched a line through Raquel's name. Then he turned and headed back toward the lodge.

"Yoo-hoo! Mr. Snowboarder Teacher Guy! Here I am!" A woman shuffled toward him as fast as her abundant layers of clothing allowed. "Sorry I'm so late," she panted. "I had some trouble figuring out all these zippers and snaps and pull strings." She gave him a beguiling smile.

Marc took a good look at the woman tucked inside the pink faux-fur lined hood. "Raquel Livingston I presume?" he asked with a twinkle in his eye. He was intrigued by the thatch of curly gray hair protruding from under the hood and the laugh lines around her eyes. Not many women her age enrolled in snowboarding classes.

"Guilty as charged," she replied. She lowered her voice to a whisper. "And more than a little bit nervous, too. I've never snowboarded before."

"So what made you sign up?" asked Marc as he took her registration slip.

"It's on my list," she replied. "You know, the things you want to do before you die?"

Marc nodded. It had been on his list too, when, at nearly 50 years of age, he'd taken up the sport. And now, a few years later, he was a certified instructor.

"There's no reason to be nervous," he assured her. Just relax and have fun." He smiled. "You're in good hands."

Raquel felt a strange rush pass clear through her. *Was this man flirting with her?* Impossible. She was over the hill... Well, almost... and certainly this man, a snowboard instructor, would be attracted to the throng of much younger women out on the slopes...

"Raquel?"

"Oops." She hoped he'd think it was just the cold turning her cheeks red. "You were saying?"

"I was saying you have nothing to worry about. I'll make sure you don't fall."

"Will you put that in writing?" Raquel laughed. No doubt about it, she was very attracted to this man.

Marc handed her a snowboard and explained the fundamentals of the sport while they walked a short ways up the gentle slope.

At the top of the small rise Marc had her step into the bindings. As he bent to adjust the straps, Raquel resisted the urge touch his shock of silver-white hair.

"Raquel? Any questions?"

"I... uh... I was just wondering how you were going to keep me from falling. I can't even walk in this get-up."

Marc grinned. "Just like this." He placed his board uphill and parallel to hers, the boards almost touching, and stepped quickly into the bindings.

Raquel could barely breathe. He was so... close.

"May I put my arms around you?" he asked.

Speechless, she nodded.

Marc placed his arms around her waist and instructed her to lean back and flex her knees. He shifted his weight slightly to the downhill side and they glided effortlessly across the snow. "Oh…" she sighed, finally taking a deep breath. "This is… wonderful!"

"Just like dancing," replied Marc, shifting their combined weight to the other edge of the board. They traversed back across the face of the hill. "All you have to do is follow my lead. Don't fight it, just go with the flow."

Raquel had no intention of fighting it. She could die right this minute and not give a diddly about doing any of the other things "on her list."

Marc maneuvered them through two more turns before they stopped at the bottom of the hill. He released his grasp, unfastened his own bindings, and stepped free. As he did so, Raquel suddenly lost her balance and unceremoniously plopped over in the snow.

Unable to pick herself up with her feet still strapped in, she waved her arms around, flailing helplessly.

Marc looked down at her. She looked so soft, so fragile… He quickly cleared his throat. "Now's probably not the best time for you to be making snow angels, Raquel," he deadpanned.

"Hey, you promised I wouldn't fall!"

"Yes, I did, didn't I?" Marc reached out both hands, and she placed her hands in his so he could set her upright. "I guess that means I owe you a cup of hot chocolate."

"Hot chocolate?" Raquel echoed.

"Ok, then dinner. Lady, you sure drive a hard bargain." Marc smiled again, checking his watch. "Meet me in the lodge dining room at 6:30. I've got to run now; my next student is already waiting."

Raquel had no doubt she'd be on time.

Planting the Seeds of Love

Under more controlled conditions, Amy didn't mind getting her hands dirty. But today's April showers had turned into a complete downpour. The Arbor Day landscaping and planting of trees in the newly created city park had become a virtual mud bath.

She stood to stretch her back and water ran off the brim of her "Save the Earth" baseball cap and down her face. Amy shook her head, and the spray flew out in every direction.

"Hey there!" A man approaching her laughed and held up his hands in self-defense. "Are you trying to drown me?"

"We may all soon be treading water," Amy replied with a smile. "What a grand Saturday for gardening!"

"At least we won't have to water the newly planted seeds and shrubbery," replied the congenial man. He pulled a flyer from the plastic zippered pouch he carried. "Put this in your pocket," he instructed. "You can read it later."

"What is it?" Amy stuck the paper in her jacket pocket without reading it.

"An invitation to the potluck for all the volunteers here today," he replied. "It has the directions to the event on it." His eyes were deep brown and his voice sent an involuntary shiver clear through her.

She nodded and self-consciously swiped the back of

her hand across her cheek. "I'm a mess," she said.

The man laughed. "There's plenty of time to clean up before the potluck—it's not till tomorrow evening." He smiled again. "I hope you'll be there," he said, before moving on to the next volunteer.

Three short blasts on the air horn a little while later signaled the volunteers to pack up their gear and return to the main parking lot. It was almost dark, and Amy was more than ready to get home to a hot shower, yet she stayed to load shovels and spades into the back of the city truck. She was hoping for a chance to speak to the handsome man with the flyers again, but he was nowhere in sight.

Disappointed, she walked home, showered, and fell into bed without bothering with dinner. By morning, Amy was ravenous, and during a hearty breakfast she convinced herself that the mysterious man was probably married anyway.

It was still raining, so Amy decided to take in an afternoon matinee at the mall cinema. As she was about to head home, she was lured by the posters in the lobby and impulsively stayed to see a second movie. By the time it was over, she'd forgotten all about the man at the park and the volunteer potluck.

The next Saturday Amy found the invitation in the pocket of her gardening jacket when she pulled it on to go visit the city park. She'd decided to see how their handiwork looked in the bright afternoon sun. Reading the flyer now, she regretted not attending the gathering, and felt remorse at her unappreciative absence.

The flyer said the potluck was hosted by Mike and Missy, and the address indicated they lived only a few blocks away. In fact, Amy could walk by the house on her way to the park if she slightly altered her route.

Amy decided to stop to express her regrets at not attending the potluck. She didn't recall meeting either Mike or Missy on planting day, so now might be a good time to get to know these other volunteers.

She found the house with no problem. Timidly, she rang the bell and was pleasantly surprised seconds later when the man who'd passed out the flyers opened the door.

"Well, well!" His smile spread clear across his face. "Better late than never?"

"I, uh, well, um..." Amy was totally tongue-tied.

The man laughed. "Please! Come in! I'm sure I can rustle us up some of the leftovers—if they aren't too fuzzy and green by now."

Amy finally found her voice, and stuck out her hand. "You must be Mike," she said. "I'm Amy."

Mike took her hand in both of his and shook it warmly. "Amy! How nice to meet you! Now please, come in!" He dropped her hand and motioned for her to enter.

"No, I couldn't," Amy began. "I didn't call first, and I wouldn't want to impose on you and your wife."

"Wife?" Mike tilted his head and looked at her quizzically.

"Missy."

"MISSY!" Mike bellowed out the name and a big golden retriever bounded into the room. "Amy, meet Missy."

Amy's face turned bright red. She crouched down and held out her hand to the dog. "Nice to meet you Missy," she said, and shook the dog's extended paw. She looked up at Mike. "A cup of coffee would be nice."

Missy happily wagged her tail and led the way to the kitchen.

Better than French Fries

Jonas strode quickly up to the fast food counter to place his order. The young woman waiting at the cash register smiled brightly and bid him a cheerful good morning.

He glanced at his watch. Eleven forty-five. "Yes," he said, nodding in agreement, "I guess it is still morning." He noted the fresh milk-stirred-into-coffee color of her skin. She looked adorable with her curly black hair gathered into an unruly ponytail protruding from the back of her Taco Heaven ball cap.

"I'll have the Fiesta Salad."

"Chicken or beef?"

"Chicken, please, with extra salsa, and a medium soda."

The woman punched in his order and waited while Jonas pulled some money from his wallet. As he handed her the ten-dollar bill, he took a good look at her nametag. "Is that your birth name or a nickname?" he inquired while she gathered his change from the till.

"My birth name."

"Z-z-a-l-e-x," Jonas spelled aloud. "How do you pronounce it?"

"Zay-lee."

"Zay-lee," repeated Jonas, nodding. "Your mother must have given you such a pretty name because she knew you'd grow up to be such a beautiful woman."

Zzalex smiled patiently as she handed him his change. "I hear that a lot."

Jonas felt his face fall. "Y-yes," he stammered, "I suppose you do."

"Your number is 2-0-8," said Zzalex, handing him his receipt. She motioned toward the pick-up sign at the far end of the counter and waited for him to step aside so the next customer could order.

Jonas didn't get the hint. Nor could he find, in his desperately struggling mind, something witty or even mildly entertaining to say in order to keep the conversation going. "Y-you didn't ask me if I wanted fries with that," he finally managed to blurt out with a forced half-chuckle.

"Sir," sighed Zzalex, "you ordered a salad."

"Yeah, well, couldn't I still g-get some fries with that?" Jonas flushed.

"Sir," Zzalex said with her practiced customer service voice, "would you like to order some fries?"

"No, I guess not." He stepped back to wait for his food and watched as Zzalex turned to give the next man in line that same dazzling smile.

"Two-zero-eight," called another woman from the far end of the counter.

Jonas collected his salad and got a plastic fork and napkin from the condiment bar. He filled his cup at the soda fountain along the wall and slumped dejectedly into a small booth by the window. Mindlessly, he ate his meal while the place filled up with the usual lunch crowd.

By the time he dumped his trash into the bin by the door, Zzalex was nowhere in sight. *Just as well,* he thought, wishing he had made a better first impression. Maybe if he came back tomorrow... But no, if he did that, she'd probably think he was stalking her.

It was a week before Jonas found the nerve to return to Taco Heaven. Zzalex was working the order counter as he timidly approached.

"You want fries with your Fiesta Salad?" That brilliant smile again.

"You remember me?" Jonas wasn't sure if that was a good thing or a bad thing.

"Sure I remember you." She batted her eyelashes at him. "But tell me… are you ready for your quiz?"

"My quiz?"

"I remembered what you ordered last week; do you remember how to say my name?"

"Zay-lee!" Jonas erupted without thinking.

"And why," she asked, coyly tipping her head to one side, "would you trouble yourself to remember my name?"

Was this some kind of trick question? Jonas hesitated, chewing on his lower lip.

"Because," Zzalex supplied the answer for him, "you wanted to be able to call me by name so you could ask me out, remember?"

Jonas gulped and nodded weakly. "S-so, will you go out with me?" he asked.

"I'll have to think about it." She giggled.

Jonas could feel the perspiration beginning to form on his forehead. "Okay." He nodded again, paid for his meal, and moved to the far end of the counter to wait. When his number was called, he moved quickly to collect the tray.

Zzalex herself handed it to him, along with his receipt. "You forgot this," she said sweetly.

Jonas looked down at the slip of paper. Handwritten on it was a phone number and the words "Call me," followed by the letter "Z" and a smiley face. He looked up.

Zzalex shrugged. "You're kinda cute," she said. "Really, really, shy, but cute." She smiled again. "I'd love to get to know you better."

Later that day, Jonas couldn't remember a thing he had eaten for lunch, but he was sure he'd never had a meal that tasted so good.

Twelve Steps to Love

Cowboys always did that to her. Give her a man in cowboy boots, tight-fitting jeans, and a tooled leather belt with a big silver buckle, and the guy instantly commanded her full attention. He didn't even need to wear the hat.

Jenna knew this man could be dangerous: six feet tall, perfectly trimmed salt and pepper hair, intense brown eyes and a smile that lit up the entire room as he walked in. He helped himself to some coffee at the counter.

She couldn't resist. "Hello Ken," she said, walking up to him and extending her hand. "I'm Jenna."

"Pleased to meet you, Jenna." That smile again. "My belt gave me away, didn't it?"

Jenna nodded. "If you want to remain truly anonymous, you'll have to forgo clothing with your name scrawled across it."

"You're assuming it's my belt."

Coffee almost spewed from Jenna's nose at his clever comeback. "Good one," she acknowledged, turning to find a seat in the small room.

Ken settled easily into the next chair. "Come here often?"

"As often as my work schedule permits," Jenna replied. "But I don't believe I've seen you here before."

"Just moved in a few weeks ago," said Ken. "Been busy getting unpacked."

Jenna nodded and remained silent.

"I bought the Andersen place out at the end of Robber's Roost."

"I know the place." Jenna smiled. "I used to go to keggers out there."

Ken raised an eyebrow.

"Don't get the wrong idea," Jenna hastily continued, "I haven't had a drink in over 15 years."

"You've got me beat by a year or two," Ken said thoughtfully. "And since neither one of us is in our first year of sobriety, I suppose no one would object to us going out for a cup of *decent* coffee after the meeting."

Jenna's heart lodged in her throat. "I suppose not," she whispered as the chairperson called for the meeting to open with the Serenity Prayer.

It was the longest hour in recorded history. Finally, the chairperson asked them to stand and form a circle. Jenna felt the warmth and safety of her hand in Ken's. She also felt a tingle of electricity extending clear down to her toes. *Whoa girl.*

After exchanging pleasantries with many familiar faces, Jenna edged toward the door. She saw Ken engaged in a lively conversation. *So much for that,* she thought, *maybe another time.* She headed for her car.

"Jenna!" called Ken, hurrying across the parking lot behind her, "You don't think you're going to get out of buying me that cup of coffee, do you?"

"*I'm* buying?"

"Well, yes, as a friendly and neighborly gesture, I was sure you'd want to pick up the tab."

Jenna stared at him in disbelief. Was he teasing, or was he some kind of ne'er-do-well mooch looking for a handout? She decided to give him the benefit of the doubt.

"I'd be happy to buy you that cup of coffee, Ken. Follow me to Mabel's Diner.

Jenna mentally awarded him points when he held the restaurant door open for her. She gave him several more points when he told the waitress they'd like a booth in the non-smoking section.

"How'd you know I don't smoke?" she asked as they were seated.

"I know a lot of things about you," he replied, giving her a mysterious wink and handing her one of the menus the hostess left on the table.

"Really?" said Jenna coquettishly. "Like what, for instance?"

"Like I know I lured you here for a cup of coffee, but since you took the menu from me without hesitation, I assume you haven't had dinner yet."

Jenna laughed. "Reflex action, I guess."

"And before you jump to the conclusion that I'm the world's biggest freeloader," he quickly went on, "I coerced you into buying the coffee because the only cash I had on me at the meeting was a dollar for the collection basket. But if you'd be so gracious as to accept a last-minute dinner invitation, I do have a viable debit card."

Jenna liked his style. She opened the menu and quickly skimmed through the offerings. "Since you presume to know so much about me," she said coyly, "just what do you think I'll order?"

At that moment, the waitress appeared to fill their coffee cups. "Are you two ready to order?" she asked.

"I'll have the homemade meatloaf special," Ken began, "cottage fries with gravy, and green salad with ranch dressing." He looked at Jenna. "And the lady will have…"

"The lady will have the same," Jenna replied softly.

"Well," remarked the waitress, "that was easy." She flipped her order pad closed. "You two certainly seem to be on the same page tonight."

"That's exactly what I was thinking," said Ken, as he placed his hand over Jenna's and squeezed.

In Perfect Harmony

"Pick her! Pick her!" Becky bounced in her chair, enthusiastically pointing to the woman seated next to her.

Marianne turned scarlet. "Stop it!" she hissed. "Cut it out!"

Becky stood up and waved her arms over her head, again calling out to the singer on the stage. "Pick her! It's her *birthday*!" She motioned at Marianne.

That got Tom's full attention. He strode toward them and reached out his hand. "Ladies and gentlemen," he said into the microphone, "how about a little encouragement to get the birthday gal up here with me."

The audience responded by applauding loudly and chanting, "Birthday girl! Birthday girl! Birthday girl!"

"I'll get you for this," said Marianne over her shoulder as she reluctantly got to her feet and accepted Tom's assistance onto the stage.

"Tell us your name," he said. He held the microphone in front of her mouth.

"M-Marianne," she said in a hoarse whisper.

"Marianne," repeated Tom. "As in…" Tom broke into song "… the professor and Marianne, here on Gilligan's Isle."

Marianne smiled weakly. Like she hadn't heard that a million times before.

"So how old are you?" he asked into the mic.

Marianne glared at him. No way was she going to admit to being 30 in front of a room full of strangers. She had only agreed to come see this casino show at the insistence of her best friend. Becky could be quite stubborn, and she had refused to take "no" for an answer, especially since it was Marianne's birthday.

Tom put an arm around her and Marianne resisted the urge to pull away. "Your good friend Becky and I have a little surprise for you," he began. "Do you like surprises?"

"Not really," Marianne sputtered in reply.

"Oh, I think you'll like this one," countered Tom. "It's made of chocolate."

A casino employee appeared from backstage carrying a large cake covered in blazing candles.

"Everybody sing!" Tom called out as he led them into a jazzed up rendition of "Happy Birthday."

Marianne caught Becky's eye in the audience. *I'm going to kill you*, she mouthed.

Becky just laughed and clapped.

Tom then instructed Marianne to make a wish and blow out the candles before the fire department arrived.

Another lame joke, thought Marianne, but she managed to blow them all out with one mighty exhale.

"I'm sure Marianne wants to share her cake," said Tom to the audience, "so you'll each be receiving a piece of it shortly. Meanwhile, I have a show to continue." He kissed Marianne on the cheek, thanked her for being a good sport, and helped her down from the stage.

Returning to the table, Marianne picked up her purse. "Let's go."

Becky didn't budge. "We haven't had any cake yet." She smiled sweetly at Marianne. "And it would be rude to leave before he finishes this set. Besides, I think he likes you. Maybe he'll join us during his break."

Marianne plopped back down into her seat. She knew it was fruitless to argue with Becky. "Swell." She sighed. "So you think I'm so desperate that I need a lounge lizard like him to ask me out?"

Becky shrugged. "Well, he is cute… Tall, dark hair, broad shoulders… And you have to admit, you haven't had a lot of offers lately."

"Gee, thanks for reminding me."

Despite her misgivings, Marianne enjoyed the rest of Tom's set, even singing along with a few of the old rock and roll standards. And the cake almost convinced her to forgive her best friend. Almost.

As Becky predicted, after Tom programmed the CD player to carry on for a few minutes without him, he pulled up a chair at their table. He handed Marianne a CD of his own music. "Happy Birthday," he said softly.

Marianne took note of the sincerity in his voice without the microphone in his hand and the fact that he wore no wedding ring almost simultaneously. "Thank you. That's very nice of you." Cheeks flaming, she examined the song list printed on the case.

"Now before you go jumping to any conclusions," said Tom, "I want you to know I'm not really a full-time lounge singer. I teach vocal music at the high school. I just work here a couple nights a week to pay off my college loans a little faster."

"Oh, I see." Marianne gave him her first genuine smile. "That's great. I'll bet you're a really good teacher."

"Well, if you two will excuse me," said Becky, standing up to leave, "I think I'll go play the slot machines for a little while. I feel lucky tonight."

Marianne gazed into Tom's deep blue eyes. *Me too!*

Serving Up Romance

Mike was still breathing heavily as he jogged slowly up the beach access road to cool down. He continued past the timing table without breaking stride. He couldn't care less how long it had taken him to complete the 10K beach run. He had finished the race; that was enough.

Approaching the folding tables set up at the end of the road, Mike slowed to a walk and picked up a bottle of water from the first one. He drained it in a few gulps and deposited the container into the recycling bin.

"Did you work up a good appetite?" asked the young woman with curly brown hair tucked up under a hairnet at the second table. She was ladling out generous portions of clam chowder for the race participants.

"It sure smells good," replied Mike, reaching out to accept a bowl from her.

"Crackers, spoons and napkins are right on down the line." She smiled pleasantly.

"Very efficient assembly line you got going here."

The woman nodded enthusiastically. "After many years, we've learned what works best for our annual 'World's Longest Beach Run and Chowder Feed'."

The line moved forward, and Mike was forced to move with it. Too late, he realized he should have asked her name. He gathered his utensils, napkin, a slice of hot garlic bread and another bottle of water before finding a seat at the picnic tables scattered about. While he ate, he kept looking back toward the chowder table, but the crowd prevented him from seeing her.

People came and went for the better part of the next hour, and Mike was still unable to make up his mind about returning to speak to the pretty brunette. Finally he stood up, walked over and dropped his trash into the nearest garbage can. *Oh well,* he sighed, *there's always next year.*

Mike proceeded leisurely up the beach approach, passing several concession stands and chatting amicably with other runners. His mind kept going back to the woman he was now fondly thinking of as "Chowder Girl." *You're just a big ol' chicken,* he chastised himself.

Abruptly, he turned and marched resolutely toward the food tables. The crowd had thinned somewhat, but he was still forced to enter the roped off area back at the first water table. Eagerly, he moved forward to the chowder table and… She was gone!

An elderly gray-haired woman had taken the brunette's place. She started to hand him a bowl of chowder, but Mike just stood there.

"Don't you like clam chowder?"

"I… uh… I love clam chowder…" Mike began. "But, I… uh… was hoping to speak to the woman who was here before." He felt his face flush.

"Do you mean Darcy?" the woman asked. "The young lady with her leg in a brace?"

"Leg in a brace?" Mike shook his head. "I didn't notice…"

"That's why she wasn't running today," the woman continued, smiling. "She had knee surgery a couple weeks ago or she would have been right out there."

The people in line behind Mike were gently pressing

him forward, and he had to move on. He ducked under the ropes and walked dejectedly away. *Snooze, you lose,* he thought sadly.

A man on a megaphone was calling for all race participants to gather under the green and white striped awning for the awards presentations. Half-heartedly, Mike joined the group assembling. He knew he hadn't "won" anything, but he wanted to support his fellow runners.

As each age category was announced, the happy winners stepped up to the podium to claim their medals, tied to red, white and blue ribbons.

"And now," said the emcee at the ceremony's conclusion, "we have some announcements." He paused, consulting his notes. "Would runner number two-zero-six-one please meet your party at the west end of the platform? Runner two-zero-six-one."

The man standing next to Mike nudged him with his elbow. "That's you, buddy."

"Me?" Mike looked down at the number pinned to his shirt. He shook his head. "That's my number," he said, "there must be some mistake." He moved against the tide of runners leaving the area and approached the podium.

"Hi!" said Darcy, beaming at him from a chair in the first row. Her leg was propped up on a second chair. "I hope you don't mind." She lowered her leg and patted the seat beside her.

Mike laughed and sat down. "That was very resourceful of you!"

She grinned. "When Mom told me someone had asked about me, she gave me the guy's entry number. I was hoping it was you."

Mike suddenly felt as though he had won the race after all.

Going Once, Going Twice...

Carly straightened up from her kneeling position, stretched her arms up over her head and arched her back. *Good thing this deck only has room for these few plant containers,* she thought. *Weeding is a lot of work!* But she smiled as she surveyed the results; it was almost like having a real garden.

She walked inside her apartment through the open sliding glass door and directly into the kitchen. Iced tea. She nodded to herself. *And the radio.* Returning to the deck, she sprawled out in the lounge chair and tuned the radio to the local public service station.

The station was sponsoring an on-air auction to benefit the Humane Society, and Carly wondered if there would be anything she'd like to bid on. On impulse, she retrieved her portable phone and set it on the small table next to her chair.

It was a warm day, and Carly dozed off. She dreamed of having her own home someday, with a big backyard and plenty of room for lots of plants and lots of adopted animals from the shelter. When she awoke, the sun was much lower in the sky and the on-air auction was coming to a close.

"We have just one more item to auction off," said the announcer, who identified himself as Humane Society Stan. "A full-service oil change from EZ Oil. Bidding will start at $10. Call now!"

My car could use an oil change, thought Carly. *And it's for a good cause.* The bidding on this one was pretty intense, no doubt bolstered by other last-minute bargain hunters. But Carly won the auction, and was told she could pick up her certificate the next day.

But the next day, when Carly arrived after work to claim her prize, she discovered there had been a mix-up. The only unclaimed certificate was for dinner for two at a very nice local restaurant.

"I don't understand how this could have happened." Stan shook his head. "Who would have won this nice dinner certificate and left here with a document entitling them to an oil change?"

"I'm sure they'll realize their mistake before too long and come back in to exchange it," said Carly. "When they do, you can call me and I'll come back in." She wrote her number down on the post-it not he'd handed her.

"Thanks for being a good sport about this," he said. Carly noticed he had a great smile, and that he wore no wedding ring.

"No problem." She returned his grin, and left feeling glad she would have another opportunity to talk with him.

Nearly three weeks passed, and no call came from Stan or anyone else at the station. *Oh well,* thought Carly, *at least no money exchanged hands.*

She had almost forgotten the whole thing when she received a note in the mail from the Humane Society thanking her for her contribution. Now, that's really odd, she mused. Pulling on her light jacket, she decided to stop in at the animal shelter and see if anyone there could shed some light on this puzzle.

Stan was sitting behind the desk with a cat on his

lap when she walked through the door. "Hello again!" he said, springing to his feet, and dislodging the cat. "Remember me? Humane Society Stan, the guest announcer for the benefit auction?"

"Yes... Uh... Hello..." stammered Carly. "I thought you worked at the radio station."

"Nope. I work right here, helping out our little animal buddies." He motioned with both arms to the general area around him. "And I'll bet you're here about that thank you note from us," he continued.

"Why, yes, that's exactly why I'm here."

"And since you never got the oil change, you're wondering why you're getting a thank you note, right?"

"Right..." Carly smiled tentatively and nodded. "Enlighten me."

"Well," said Stan, looking mighty pleased with himself, "no one ever came back in to claim the restaurant certificate, so I bought it myself. But I put your name down as the donor."

"So I owe you for a dinner certificate?"

"No, no, of course not..." Stan shook his head and grinned again. "But I would very much like you to join me in using it—What night are you free for dinner?"

Carly laughed. She liked his style, but— "I hardly know you," she began.

"Do you need references? Everyone in here will vouch for the quality of my character." His eyes sparkled as his smile deepened.

Carly realized that she would very much like to get to know him better. And it was obvious he loved animals. Maybe, she'd discover over dinner, that he also liked to garden. She looked at her watch. "As a matter of fact," she said, "I'm free tonight...."

Playing the Part

Sylvia Avery had no intention of ever climbing up onto the community theater stage, but here she was, doing just that, mounting the stairs with trembling knees.

"No pressure, Syl," called out the director. "We just need you to stand in for Annie during rehearsal tonight. She's out with laryngitis. We need your help so the other actors can get their cues from you. You can read right from the script."

Yes, thought Syl, *I can read right from the script I WROTE.* Writing was something Sylvia knew she did well. But stumbling around on the stage while delivering the dialogue was way out of her comfort zone.

And to make matters worse, over the past few weeks of rehearsals she had developed a huge crush on Russ, the actor playing the leading role. Now she was going to be reading the lines addressed to him by the character playing his wife. *Oh, swell!*

Try as she might, Sylvia was at a loss to remember where she was to stand and when she was to sit while delivering her lines. The other actors graciously pointed in the right direction or made some other motion to get her to move into the correct position.

During the break between the first and second acts, Russ approached her. "Hey, Sylvia," he said, nonchalantly running his fingers through his curly dark hair, "I didn't know you were an aspiring actor."

Sylvia blushed uncontrollably. "I— I'm not" she stammered. "I'd be too afraid of forgetting my lines in front of an audience."

Russ scowled at her. "How could you forget the lines you wrote?" he asked with genuine surprise. "Haven't you got the whole play pretty much memorized by now?"

"Not the whole play," admitted Syl. "And I've never even stood on a stage before tonight."

"Never?"

"Never." Sylvia shook her head. "I'm afraid I just couldn't handle that kind of stress."

Russ shrugged, and walked away with a puzzled expression on his face. He took his place on the set for Act Two without even saying good-bye.

Sylvia went through the motions of the second act mentally chastising herself for not coming across more charming, more witty, and certainly more entertaining in her brief conversation with Russ. Surely he must think her a total idiot for being so self-conscious and shy.

The director had several suggestions to share with them during the break between the second and third acts, and there was no chance for Sylvia to make a better impression on Russ. Disappointed, she moved to sit on the couch at center stage for the start of the next scene. Determined to make the best of it, she sat up straight and took a deep breath, hoping to gain his approval by her "can-do" spirit.

Although she was reading directly from the script, by this time Sylvia was a little more at ease with the whole process. Much to her surprise, she found herself enjoying the experience, and was almost sorry when the final curtain closed.

As the other actors gathered onstage for further comments from the director, Russ plopped himself down on the couch next to Syl. "Come here often?" he joked.

"Only when there's a good play in town," she replied, happy that she had come up with a quick and appropriate retort.

"Well, there's a good one playing now," he said. "And I happen to know the writer personally."

Sylvia blushed again, and said nothing. She wondered what it was about this guy that rendered her speechless.

"In fact," Russ continued, "I've got an idea for a sequel I think she might like. It involves the playwright and the leading man getting to know each other a little better."

Sylvia's mouth suddenly went dry.

"Of course," Russ went on with a smile, "with the playwright's permission, I'd like to make a few suggestions for the dialogue."

"Suggestions for the dialogue?" Sylvia murmured.

"Yes," said Russ, "I'd like to suggest that when the dashing leading man asks the beautiful and talented playwright to go out with him for coffee, that she enthusiastically jumps up and says, 'Yes, Russ, I'd love to!"

The humor cut through the awkwardness of the moment and Sylvia grinned at him. Spontaneously, she jumped to her feet. "Yes, Russ, I'd love to!" she parroted.

Sylvia was startled by the applause of the other actors who had not yet left the stage.

"You certainly take direction well," laughed the director. "Perhaps you'll want to try out for a part in your next play after all."

Perhaps I will, thought Syl, already beginning to formulate a romantic plotline in her head. *Perhaps I will.*

Suited to a Tee

Marie stared at the community college enrollment form. "You signed me up for a physical education class?" she asked in disbelief.

"It's a beginning golf class," exuded Tracy. "Starts next Tuesday, right after work. You'll get fresh air and exercise at the same time. You'll love it."

"I won't *'love it'*." Marie attempted to hand the paper back to her best friend. "I'm not going."

"We're *both* going," corrected Tracy. "You think I'd sign you up for something I wouldn't do myself?" She smiled slyly. "Besides, the class is held at the country club. Think of all the eligible men we'll meet."

Marie rolled her bright blue eyes. "Well," she said slowly, "maybe we could have dinner at the club restaurant after class."

Tracy beamed. She handed Marie a brochure. "You should probably know the difference between a fairway and a green before we get there."

"A what and a who?"

Tracy scooted out the door before Marie could change her mind.

On Tuesday afternoon, the two young women signed in at the pro shop and were each handed a putter. "This is all you'll need for today's lesson," said the woman at the counter. "The putting green is around back."

Marie and Tracy joined 13 other women, ages ranging from 25 to 65, all standing awkwardly around the instructor. "You were *so* right," whispered Marie, "we'll meet a lot of eligible men in this class."

Tracy scowled at her, but said nothing. Soon the two became totally absorbed in learning to putt. After class, they both felt a sense of accomplishment.

"Ok, admit it," said Tracy. "You had fun today."

"Yes, I did, thank you," Marie replied. "Especially when I made a good putt."

The following week's golf lesson was at the practice bunker. "Today you make friends with your wedge," the instructor began.

Marie took her place in line and watched as each woman got five chances to pop a golf ball out of the sand trap.

"Ladies! Ladies! Line up again," the instructor cheerily called out. "We'll keep working on this until we've all experienced success."

Nearly an hour later, Tracy and Marie settled themselves into chairs in the country club's small bistro. "Can you believe that guy?" asked Tracy, scanning the menu. "I think he actually meant it when he said he'd hold the flashlight for us if it got too dark."

Marie giggled. "Well, after his comment, your shots certainly improved!"

They fell into a fit of laughter just as two men approached their table. "Excuse us," began the taller man, "but we couldn't help noticing you both had a little difficulty out there today."

"You couldn't help noticing?" Tracy replied. "Just what does *that* mean?"

"We weren't stalking you or anything," said the

shorter, sandy-haired man hastily. "We were relaxing on the bistro's deck after our golf game and there's a good view of the practice area." He pointed through the sliding glass door. "My name's Jack," he continued, "and this is my friend Edward."

After introductions all around, Edward spoke again. "You're taking the college class, aren't you?" The women nodded. "Then next week you'll be on the driving range."

"If you say so." Marie finally found her voice.

"It's the same every quarter," replied Jack. "You learn the fundamentals, then put it all together the last session to actually play a complete round." He smiled.

"We were just wondering," said Edward, "if maybe you ladies would like a head start on next week's lesson and get together with us on the driving range later this week."

"We'd love to," enthused Tracy, before Marie could stop her.

Jack and Edward both exhaled with genuine relief. "How about Thursday afternoon then?" asked Edward. "Five o'clock okay?"

"We'll look forward to it," said Tracy, again responding for them both.

The men left them to enjoy their dinner. Tracy pretended not to notice Marie glaring at her. "What?" she finally asked. "Don't you want to get in some extra driving practice? It couldn't hurt to get some tips from a couple of very nice guys who just so happen to already play the game."

"That sweet and innocent look will not work on me," Marie tried to admonish her, then shrugged. "But you're right. We could use the additional help."

Tracy grinned. "And Jack is really cute."

"Not as cute as Edward," replied Marie, also

smiling.

"Well," laughed Tracy, "at least neither one of them is named 'Chip'."

"Chip? Who's Chip?"

"May I suggest," said Tracy, still laughing, "that you study those golf terms more thoroughly before Thursday? I was making a joke about a chip shot."

Marie smiled good-naturedly, enjoying the tingle of excitement as she thought about Thursday's extra practice. Golfing might be a good way to meet men after all.

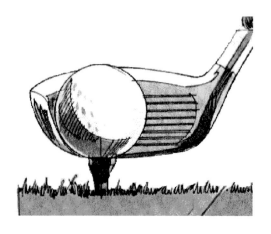

Late-breaking News

"Lucky you," said Trish, handing a *Tinkerville Tribune* assignment card to her best friend. "Guess which ace reporter gets to cover the second graders' Groundhog Day assembly this morning?"

"Oh, swell." Delia read over the card she'd been handed. "Gordy the Groundhog is going to explain why not seeing his shadow is a prediction of an early spring. This isn't exactly what we'd call 'breaking news' is it?"

"Don't be so impatient," replied Trish. "It took me three years to work up from obituaries to hard news. Community service writing is a good place to start." She smiled at Delia. "And who knows? Your writing assignments are getting you out into the public eye. With your long auburn hair framing that cute little freckled face of yours, it's only a matter of time before you bump into Prince Charming. Maybe today will be the day."

Delia tucked the card in her pocket and checked her watch before picking up notepad and camera. "Not too many eligible men teach in the primary grades, but I'll keep my eyes open."

"Keep an open mind, too," Trish called out as Delia left the office. "You just never know."

For some reason, Delia had assumed that an animal handler, perhaps someone working for the local zoo, would be bringing a live groundhog to the school for the kids to see. As it turned out, "Gordy the Groundhog" was a six foot tall human in a very furry costume. Delia couldn't help but smile as she snapped several photos of the kids tentatively "petting" the costumed man before the presentation.

"The groundhog is also known by the names 'woodchuck' and 'whistlepig'," said Gordy, "but today is Groundhog Day. And this morning, my famous cousin, Punxsutawney Phil, was on the national news. Today Phil saw his shadow. Who knows what that means?" Most of the small hands in the room waved excitedly in the air, hoping to be called on.

Delia sat back and enjoyed the show. She thought maybe she should be writing a science report instead of a human interest feature. The man was amazing the way he wove a myriad of facts about groundhogs into his entertaining stories.

As the children all applauded, Delia gathered up her writing tools. She followed the lines of students out of the auditorium and turned toward the parking lot. A furry hand touched her shoulder.

"Excuse me, uh, Miss?" said Gordy the Groundhog. "It *is* Miss, isn't it?"

Delia was slightly startled, but recovered quickly. She stuck out her hand. "Miss Walton. Delia Walton. Reporter for the *Tinkerville Tribune*. That was a fine educational program you presented."

Gordy shook her hand. "Would you like an exclusive?" he asked. "We could have coffee and—"

"No thank you," she said more curtly than necessary. "I was here to cover a story, and now I need to go write it up. I'm on deadline. And, just for the record," she paused to smile disarmingly, "I am *not* in the habit of having coffee with rodents." Then she turned and strode purposefully from the building.

"You actually said that?!" asked an incredulous Trish when Delia recounted her morning. "Why didn't you give the guy a shot? You never know when Mr. Right will show up *or* what he'll be wearing."

"I guess he just caught me off-guard," replied Delia. "He had amazing dark brown eyes, but what kind of a future does a guy have who impersonates groundhogs for a living?"

With that, Delia got busy at her keyboard. She had just about an hour before she was due to cover the dedication of the new hospital wing and then a special school board meeting luncheon. The thought of covering yet another meeting did nothing for her appetite, but at least today she'd get to have a lunch break.

Promptly at noon, Delia slid into one of the unoccupied chairs at the back of the room and arranged her notepad next to her salad plate. The school board chairperson was just beginning his opening remarks.

"It is our great pleasure today," he intoned, "to officially welcome our new Superintendent. He arrived a few weeks ago, but he's been so busy enmeshing himself in the community that we had to put off formally introducing him until today. Please welcome Gordon Albright."

Polite applause accompanied Mr. Albright to the podium. He took a moment to survey the room, his eyes lighting on Delia. He smiled, and took a sip of water. "Yes, indeed, I've been quite a busy boy since I arrived."

He smiled again, looking right at her. "One of the things I like best about a school district this small is the opportunity I have to be a real 'hands on' administrator. Just this morning I got to dip into my biology background and give a little lecture to the second grade classes on groundhogs."

Delia thought the heat from her face would set the tablecloth on fire. It was too late to slink out the door without causing a stir, and she knew she had to file this story before she finished for the day, so leaving was out of the question.

"Frequent classroom visits help me keep in touch with how the curriculum is meeting the needs of our students," the new superintendent continued.

She tried to focus on what he was saying about his future plans for the neighborhood schools. In all her life, Delia could not remember being more embarrassed or more uncomfortable.

"I can't believe it!" exclaimed Trish when Delia told her friend about her second encounter with Gordy the Groundhog. "What were the odds on *that* happening?"

"This just hasn't been my day," said Delia, shaking her head ruefully. "At least I've gotten all my stories filed early so that now I can head home and take my mind off my troubles in a nice hot bath."

"Hot baths are great for reducing stress," said a man standing at the front counter of the newspaper office. Delia didn't have to look up to recognize the voice. "But so is joining me for dinner at a quiet relaxing restaurant."

Delia met his eyes and quickly scrutinized the man before her. Smart, funny, apparently very forgiving, and certainly persistent. She gave Gordon her best smile. "I'd love to," she said, picking up her purse and leaving her reporter's notepad on the desk.

It was hard to believe the groundhog had seen his shadow that very morning; Delia could sense that a wonderful spring was right around the corner.

You are My Sunshine

Denise looked around the middle school choir room and sighed. Her entire class, all 47 of her general music students now entering the room and taking their seats, were wearing some combination of black, gray, or navy blue. *How dull,* she thought, *how drab.*

She gazed out the window. Rain coursed against the pane. The November sky was gray, the wet parking lot was gray, most of the cars parked there were gray, even the grass and the trees looked gray. Gray seagulls hovered in the air near the industrial gray garbage cans. Denise sighed again. How she longed for spring!

"Ms. Griswald?" A voice interrupted her reverie.

"Yes, Donald?" She smiled warmly at her newest student. Donald had joined the class in mid-October, a full six weeks after the beginning of the school year. Denise suspected he was placed in her general chorus not by choice, but because it was one of the last elective classes with any openings this semester.

"Ms. Griswald, it's about those songs we're practicing for the Harvest Festival."

"Yes? What about them?"

"Well, I was wondering if maybe we could also sing something my mother used to sing to me."

Denise paused to study the earnest young man standing before her. She knew that his father had been transferred to this community with the Coast Guard. She had met the handsome man in uniform just briefly when Donald enrolled, but she didn't know any other specifics of his home situation.

"A song your mother *used* to sing to you?"

"Yes, Ma'am. My mother died of cancer last year. She used to sing to me all the time before she got too sick." Donald's gaze dropped to the floor, and his voice became little more than a mumble. "Most everybody probably already knows her favorite song. It would mean a whole lot to me if you would consider us singing it."

Denise's throat felt like she had a brick stuck in it. She put a protective arm around Donald's shoulders. "I'll see what we can do," she promised him.

The next two weeks flew by. The end of the first quarter, with grade reports to complete, parent conferences to attend, and preparations for the Harvest Festival to oversee, Denise was kept hopping. All too soon, it was the day of the school concert.

"Now remember," she instructed her chorus class, "I want to see you all here at least 15 minutes early tonight. Girls in dresses. Boys in slacks, not jeans, and a nice long-sleeved button-down shirt."

Her pronouncement was met with loud groans from the majority of the student body. "No arguments. No exceptions. You've known for weeks what was required for this performance, and I look forward to seeing you all in your Sunday best." Denise wondered if anyone listening knew what "Sunday best" used to mean. She also wondered if anyone was actually listening, but quickly dismissed that thought.

At promptly 6:45 that evening, Denise took attendance. Donald was the only one missing. She frowned, wishing she had thought to ask him if he needed to borrow a long-sleeved shirt from the drama department's prop room. She shrugged it off and began leading the vocal warm-up exercises.

A scant five minutes before show time, Donald burst into the room. "Sorry I'm late, Ms. G," he hastened to explain. "My dad had to work late again, and we almost didn't make it. We didn't even have time for dinner." He took off his coat, slung it over the back of a chair and took his place on the choir risers.

The room became still as his classmates stared at him in open-mouth silence. There, among the dreary dresses and non-descript shirts, Donald's bright yellow shirt stood out like a flaming daffodil in an otherwise sea of darkness.

"Quick! Somebody! Get me my sunglasses!" bellowed one of the rowdier boys.

"He's so bright his father calls him Sun!" quipped another.

"They call him Mellow Yellow," said a third student, not wanting to be outdone.

"That's quite enough, ladies and gentlemen." Denise clapped her hands sharply. "I happen to think Donald's shirt is most appropriate for our final selection this evening." She smiled just for him as she turned to lead her students down the hallway and into the combination gymnasium/auditorium.

The beginning band students played first. Then the jazz band wowed the audience with songs that rocked the rafters. After the jazz band, the select "Chordettes," a group of 20 especially talented girls, sang a few classy show tunes. Then finally, the general chorus took the stage.

Denise scanned the students standing before her.

She could imagine how sweaty some of their palms must be. She gave them a grin and a double thumbs up, then turned to address the crowd.

Instantly, she recognized Donald's father. Although he had not made it to conference night, due to his work schedule, there was no mistaking the family resemblance. That and the fact that he was the only man in the auditorium besides Donald who also wore a bright yellow shirt! Denise caught his eye and smiled warmly as she introduced herself to the audience.

The chorus sang beautifully, and the conclusion of each number was met with hearty applause. "For our finale tonight," said Denise into the microphone, "I'd like to invite all of you to join us in singing an American classic. This song is an oldy but goody, and reminds us that even during winter gray skies, there is still much to be thankful for. Please join us in singing You Are My Sunshine."

Denise turned and directed the pianist to begin the introduction, then led the chorus, assisted by the audience, through its final number. At the conclusion, many parents came forward to shake her hand and offer their congratulations and praise for a job well done. Swamped by well-wishers, Denise lost track of Donald and his father.

Two dozen daffodils graced Denise's desk the next morning. There was a note with the flowers that read: *I now understand why my son speaks so highly of you. Thank you for being so kind to him. I will be picking him up from school this afternoon and would like to invite you for coffee, if you're not too busy. Sincerely, Donald's Dad.*

Denise felt warm all over as she checked her school calendar. It was still many months until spring, she noted. But for today, she could be absolutely certain she was not too busy for coffee and a bit of sunshine.

No Roadblocks to Love

Susan's headlights illuminated the barrier blocking the dark roadway ahead of her. A police car was parked next to it. She slowed to a stop and rolled down her window for the patrolman who approached.

"Evening, Miss," said the officer, nodding his head briefly as water coursed off the brim of his plastic-covered uniform hat. "All this rain has caused a major landslide at milepost 43, and the highway is closed for the time being."

"What about Highway 6?" asked Susan.

"That highway is closed as well, completely flooded."

"So how do I get home?" asked Susan

"I'm afraid you won't be getting home tonight," he replied. "Until t the roadway's cleared tomorrow morning and repair any damage, looks like you're stranded."

Stranded? Susan could see the police officer's lips moving, but she couldn't quite wrap her mind around what he was saying.

"Do you have any friends in the area?" he asked.

Susan shook her head. She was still over 40 miles from her rural home, and her social circle didn't extend quite this far.

"I hate to be the bearer of even more bad news," the officer continued, "but we've had a report that both motels in the little burg you just passed through are already full."

Susan was relieved to discover that what she still *could* wrap her mind around was the fact that the patrolman had gorgeous deep brown eyes and an equally gorgeous shock of curly brown hair protruding from beneath the bill of his rain hat.

She smiled despite herself, and tried to consider her options. At the moment she couldn't think of any.

"Miss? You can't park here in the middle of the road."

"Well," said Susan hesitantly, "could I park over there—" she pointed to the side of the pavement, "behind your car?"

"You want to sleep in your car by the side of the road tonight?"

Susan nodded. "It's not illegal or anything, is it?"

The officer looked puzzled, but didn't say anything.

"I'd be perfectly safe parked out here, as long as you're on duty, right?"

"Well, yes, of course, but…" he looked stymied for a moment. "Do you have a blanket or anything with you?"

"I have a pretty warm coat," replied Susan.

"Well, then I guess you can pull your car over onto the shoulder." He stepped away from her vehicle.

Susan rolled up her window and maneuvered her car as far off the roadway as she could, shut off the headlights and turned off the key.

The officer, meanwhile, was rummaging in the trunk of his patrol car. He found what he was looking for, and came back to Susan's vehicle. She opened the window again and he handed her an emergency blanket. "Here," he said, "this should help. And by the way, my name's Mike Romanski."

Thank you, Officer Mike," said Sylvia, giving him

her best smile. "I'm Susan Adams."

Mike nodded to her and touched the brim of his hat. "Pleased to meet you Susan Adams. If you need anything, just flash your lights, okay?"

Yes sir," said Susan. "And thanks again." She rolled the window up a second time and watched him get back into his car, then reclined the seat as far as it would go and pulled the blanket up around her shoulders. For a time, she watched as the intermittent cars approached, the drivers stopping to speak with Mike, and then turning their cars around and heading back into town. After what seemed like hours, Susan finally dozed.

She was awakened by a rapping on her car window. Startled, it took her a moment to realize where she was. It was just getting daylight and the rain had stopped. She quickly put the seat back up and rolled down her window.

"Good morning, Susan," said Officer Mike. "I'm going off duty now and I need to take my blanket with me." He paused as she wrestled the blanket, wrapped around her like a cocoon. "And I have some good news for you."

Susan managed a smile as she succeeded in pulling the blanket off and handing it to him. "Good news?"

"The road will be cleared in another hour or so," Mike continued. "And there's a diner a few miles back serving hot coffee and a great breakfast," he said. "Would you like to join me?"

Susan's smiled deepened. "Yes," she said, "I believe I would."

As she started her car and waited for Mike to lead the way, Susan looked into the rearview mirror, ran her fingers through her short curly hair, and popped a breath mint into her mouth. "There's all kinds of good news today, isn't there?" she said to her reflection.

How Sweet It Is

Mitchell examined the fudge samples offered by the pretty young woman in the mall's specialty candy shop. He liked to go there on Friday nights, sometimes to see a movie, and sometimes just to people watch before going home to dinner for one.

"Mmm..." he said, sniffing the air above the homemade candy. "It's hard to decide."

Amy smiled. "I get that a lot."

Mitchell nodded. "I bet you do." He finally chose a small piece of the chocolate peanut butter fudge and popped it into his mouth.

"We're having a sale on all our fudge varieties this weekend," said Amy in her polished salesclerk voice. "A dollar off per pound, or a dollar and a half off per pound for any order totaling five or more pounds."

Mitchell whistled. "Five pounds is a lot of fudge."

"It's Mother's Day weekend." Amy lowered her voice and leaned closer to him, "But I'll bet there's a lot of fudge being stashed away by adult children during this sale."

Mitchell liked the way she smelled—like jasmine, or maybe honeysuckle. Her perfume, punctuated by the aroma of so much fudge, was quite intoxicating. He started to ask her name, but before he could say a word, another man bustled up to the sample table.

Amy greeted him by name. "Hi, Evan! So nice to see

you again. Would your mother like another pound of peppermint fudge?"

"I did the math," said Evan, taking his wallet from his back pocket, "and I decided on the full five-pound assortment." He grinned. "And I'd like that wrapped in two separate boxes, please."

"Good move," said Amy. "One for your mother and one for..."

"And one for my imaginary friend," said Evan with a laugh.

Mitchell watched Evan while Evan watched Amy wrap the two boxes of fudge. Was Evan interested in more than the candy? Was Amy always that friendly with her customers? Mitchell felt a slight twinge of jealousy as Amy tucked an extra piece of cranberry fudge into Evan's carton.

As soon as Evan left with his purchase, Mitchell quickly stepped back up to the counter. "I'd like a pound of rocky road, and a pound of vanilla orange cream."

"With or without walnuts?" asked Amy, already putting paper liners into the appropriately sized boxes.

"Without, please."

Mitchell watched her hands while she worked. When she pulled off her food-handlers' gloves, he noticed she wore no rings on any finger, but that might just be an occupational preference.

"Will there be anything else?" She smiled sweetly at him.

What Mitchell really wanted was her phone number, but he was afraid that might sound too creepy.

He shook his head. "Not today, thanks." He wanted to look back as he left the store, but he didn't want to know if she wasn't wistfully watching him leave.

All Saturday morning Mitchell kicked himself for not

asking her name. Late afternoon, he drove to the mall, trying to think of some good excuse for returning to the candy shop. He certainly couldn't say he'd run out of fudge already!

"Hi Mitchell!" said Amy as soon as he entered the store. "It's good to see you again!"

Startled, Mitchell stopped in his tracks. Then he grinned—he'd used his credit card last night, and she'd remembered his name. Maybe that's how she'd known Evan's name, too. Things were looking up.

"I'm afraid you have me at a disadvantage," he said.

She pulled off her right glove and held out her hand. "Amy."

"Amy," Mitchell repeated. He liked the way her hand fit in his. "Amy."

"That's right," she said, her smile lighting up her entire face. "Or you could call me what everyone else does."

Mitchell hadn't dated in some time, but he was certain she was flirting with him. Regrettably, he let go of her hand. "And what does everyone else call you?"

"Why, The Candy Lady, of course!" Her laugh was melodious and charming.

"Of course." Mitchell was at a loss for words. He'd prepared a silly little story about accidentally forgetting to buy any fudge for his favorite aunt as an excuse to return to the shop, but now Amy had gone and made his invented tale totally unnecessary.

"Did you go and eat up both those pounds of fudge?" she asked teasingly.

"No... I... uh..."

"Good!" beamed Amy. "Then you really did come back just to see me."

Mitchell's face flushed.

Amy looked up at the clock and took off her apron. "It's closing time, Mitchell. Would you like to have a cup of coffee with me so we could get to know each other?"

Still speechless, Mitchell nodded enthusiastically.

"Sweet!" said Amy, slipping into her jacket, and Mitchell was certainly inclined to agree.

The Color of Love

"What will it be?" asked the older gentleman behind the deli counter.

Sherry ordered a toasted ham and cheese sandwich with a mountain of veggies piled on. Then she moved along toward the cash register without paying much attention to the man serving her. Her stomach growled embarrassingly loud as she reached for the bills tucked into her jeans' pocket.

"Sounds like you're getting lunch just in time," said the congenial sandwich-maker-turned-cashier.

"Yes," Sherry agreed, handing him the money. "I've worked up quite an appetite this morning."

The man started to hand back her change, then suddenly withdrew his hand. "I'm sorry, I forgot to ask you if there'd be anything else."

Sherry looked at him more closely, and was surprised to see the smiling face of a man she taught with at the high school before they both retired.

"Del!" she exclaimed. "How nice to see you!"

"And you, too, Sherry." His smiled was warm and genuine, and his eyes sparkled just as they always had in the staff room when she'd been too timid to start any kind of conversation.

A slightly awkward pause followed, until Del filled it in by saying, "So *will* there be anything else?"

"No, thank you," said Sherry. "Just the sandwich."

"You sure?" asked Del, his face taking on a slightly teasing expression.

Was he flirting with her? Sherry felt her face flush.

Del continued, "You sure you don't want some paint thinner or anything?"

"Paint thinner!" Sherry gasped and her hand self-consciously flew to her face. Then she looked down at her clothes, generously speckled with paint.

Del laughed, a deep, resonating laugh that filled the room. "It's easy to see how you worked up your appetite today." He placed her change in her hand. "What have you been painting?"

Sherry glanced behind her; there were no customers waiting in line at the moment. "I've been volunteering at the community theater," she replied.

"And let me guess," he said, "you're painting the theater pink?"

"Pink Panther Pink." Sherry laughed. "In all my 30 years teaching, I never taught drama, so I'm learning all kinds of new things at the playhouse."

"And I'm learning all kinds of ways to make a killer sandwich," said Del, with another one of his infectious laughs. "But it keeps me out meeting people, and I have a good time here."

A young couple with a child entered the deli. Sherry picked up the plastic bag holding her sandwich and headed for the door a little reluctantly. "I really do need to get back. The play opens in a week."

Del waved good-bye, and turned quickly to his next customers.

The next day Sherry decided she might have to have another sandwich from that deli for lunch. This time she took a few extra minutes to wipe the paint off her face before she went out in public.

But Del wasn't behind the counter, and Sherry felt a rush of disappointment. At the cash register, she tried to make her voice sound nonchalant. "Where's Del today?"

"Del only works two days a week. Would you like to leave a message?" asked the perky young woman waiting on her.

Sherry declined, and took her ham and cheese back to the theater to eat with the other volunteers in the Green Room.

The next few days went by in a blur, and Sherry didn't have enough time to stop by the deli. She wished she'd thought to ask which two days Del worked.

Late Friday afternoon the theater buzzed with excitement. When the last chair was finally set into place for opening night, Sherry had just enough time to get home, shower, and dress before the curtain went up.

There was something magical about the theater at night, and Sherry smiled to herself as she slid into a seat at the back of the auditorium. Even though she'd seen most of the rehearsals, she looked forward to seeing the show as strictly an audience member.

"Is anyone sitting here?"

Sherry looked up and her heart gave a little flutter. "Hi, Del. Have a seat."

He slid onto the chair next to her, leaned over and whispered, "I almost didn't recognize you without your make-up on."

"My make-up!" Sherry's hand flew to her cheek again.

Del laughed. "Just teasing," he admitted.

Her face turned a deep crimson.

"But pink is definitely your color."

Sherry's stomach rumbled in response.

"And you didn't have time for dinner tonight, did you?" he asked.

She shook her head.

"Good," said Del. "Then you won't have any excuse for not having a late supper with me after the show."

The house lights dimmed as she opened her mouth to respond.

"Shhhh..." said Del, lightly touching her hand. "We can talk later."

Sherry could hardly wait.

For a Good Cause

Nancy Grant could only think of about a thousand things she'd rather be doing on a sunny spring Saturday afternoon, but her niece had sounded desperate.

"Please, Auntie!" Marcie had begged. "I've got a test in biology on Monday, and I need the time to study."

So Nancy, being ever the good aunt, was now dressed in soggy sneakers and slacks, soaping up the front hood of yet another vehicle, filling in for Marcie at the "Safe and Sane Senior Graduation Party" fundraiser.

It looked like a lot of other seniors had found replacement volunteers as well. Nancy saw no less than 14 other adults, most with graying hair, rolling up their sleeves and pitching in at four different car-washing stations.

"Thank you for your generous donation!" called out the woman cheerily collecting the cash from each car window.

"Why hello Nancy," said the woman, as she approached her. "What a nice surprise to see you here."

Nancy bobbed her head and kept on sudsing. "Hello Mrs. Vandermere."

"You aren't in high school anymore, Nancy," laughed Mrs. Vandermere. "You may call me Estelle now."

Nancy finished the hood and stepped back so the elderly gentleman manning the hose could rinse.

"Well, Estelle," said Nancy, glancing around at all

the adults in attendance, "it looks like some things never change. I remember getting my mom to take my place at this very fundraiser just a few years ago."

Estelle laughed again. "What goes around, comes around!" And the always-energetic Senior Class Advisor was off to merrily collect from another car entering the school parking lot.

Nancy walked over to the volunteers' refreshment table and helped herself to a cookie and some soda.

"Nancy? Nancy Grant?" a booming voice said behind her.

She turned to stare into a pair of dark chocolate brown eyes.

"You probably don't remember me–" the voice continued.

Remember him? How could she not remember him? She'd sat behind him in history class their whole senior year, hoping against hope he'd someday turn around and notice her.

Nancy quickly swallowed her bite of cookie. "Hello, Tim. Nice to see you."

Tim beamed. "So you *do* remember me!" He reached for a cookie of his own. "I was so shy back in school I never worked up the nerve in school to say hello."

Nancy took a quick sip of her soda to cover her surprise.

Mrs. Vandermere clapped her hands to attract their attention. "Come on, you two, you can catch up later," she called out. "We have cars waiting!"

Nancy laughed and lowered her voice. "Doesn't she make you feel like we're still in high school?"

Tim nodded and finished off his cookie with a last bite. Brushing his hands off on his jeans, he left her to return to his group working on the far side of the lot. Nancy watched him walk away, wishing she'd come up with something witty to say in their brief encounter.

The 1 to 4 p.m. car wash still had customers waiting at 4 o'clock, so Nancy volunteered to stay a little longer, as did a handful of others. Tim, unfortunately, was nowhere to be seen.

When there were no more cars waiting, the hardy group started winding up the hoses and putting the buckets into the back of Mrs. Vandermere's pickup.

A red Mustang pulled into the lot, the driver honking the horn several times. But instead of pulling up to the washing station, the car parked next to those of the volunteers.

Tim jumped out of the car with an armload of fresh flowers. Nancy felt her cheeks turning beet red as he walked in her direction. But instead of handing them to her, he presented the huge bouquet to Mrs. Vandermere.

"Estelle," he said, "I just wanted to thank you for all you've done over the years for the graduating classes." The small crowd applauded their approval.

Then he turned to Nancy. "I never did ask you how you happened to be here today," he said quietly as the others left.

"I was filling in for my niece," said Nancy, "since it was for a good cause and all."

"Hhhmmm," said Tim. "My nephew is the one who asked me to help out today. He said he needed to study for his biology test with his girlfriend."

"His girlfriend wouldn't happen to be named Marcie, would she?" asked Nancy, quickly putting two and two together.

"Bingo," replied Tim, laughing. "But it was Mrs.

Vandermere who suggested they find able-bodied replacements if they couldn't make it today."

"You don't suppose she suggested us specifically?"

Tim shrugged. "Maybe, maybe not. Either way, she deserves those flowers."

Nancy readily agreed. She also readily agreed to dinner with Tim later that night.

A Slightly Hypothermic Christmas Eve

"It's a cute outfit, Syl," said Anna Marie, "but I still think it's a dumb idea."

"That's because you've got absolutely no imagination," replied Sylvia. She primped in front of the full-length mirror, turning this way and that, admiring herself from every angle.

"At least I have a modicum of humility," said Anna Marie under her breath.

"I heard that."

"Of course you did," said Anna Marie, helping herself to another cup of coffee. "You have selective hearing. You only hear exactly what you want to hear."

Sylvia shot "the look" at her best friend. She fluffed the white fur accentuating her cleavage and along the very short hem. She checked for the umpteenth time to make sure her black garter belt wasn't showing. "You've gotta admit it—I'm adorable."

Anna Marie nearly choked on her drink. "Yeah, yeah, whatever, you're adorable."

"Come on, say it like you mean it."

"Okay, fine. That's the cutest, sexiest, most adorable, seductive, altogether raunchy and totally slutty Santa's Little Helper costume I've ever seen."

Sylvia beamed. "Now, that's more like it!"

"But I still think it's a dumb idea."

"What's so dumb about it?"

"Well, let me be sure I've got this straight," replied Anna Marie. "You want me to drive you to Bill's house tonight, just before he gets home from work, and leave you on his front porch, dressed like this."

"Yep, that's the plan," said Syl. "I don't want him to be tipped off by seeing my car parked in his driveway."

"And what if you freeze to death before he gets home?"

"Bill's the most punctual guy I know," said Sylvia. "You can set a watch by his routine. He gets off work at 5:00, and by 5:20, he's pulling into the driveway. And besides," she continued with a sly smile, "I'll have this to keep me warm." She proudly unrolled the biggest red and white Christmas stocking Anna Marie had ever seen. "BILL" was embroidered across the top in letters almost a foot high.

"Wowza," said Anna Marie. "Where'd you get something like that?"

"On eBay, of course."

"Of course."

"So when you drop me off, I'll just snuggle into this stocking and be standing on the porch waiting for him. It's a masterpiece of an idea."

"If you say so," replied Anna Marie.

"I say so." Sylvia took a quick look at the clock on the wall. "It's almost show time," she said. "Just one more quick trip to the bathroom and I'll be all set."

Anna Marie pulled on her warm ski jacket and flipped up the hood. "You mind if I take the last bit of coffee?" she called out.

"Go right ahead," answered Syl from the bathroom. "I'm sure I'll be staying at Bill's house tonight, so flip the pot off, will you?"

Anna Marie did as she was told and gathered up her purse and car keys. Sylvia joined her in the kitchen with the sleeping bag stocking bootie draped over her arm. "Where's your coat?" asked Anna Marie.

"Don't need one," replied Sylvia, slipping into a pair of scarlet stilettos and donning a furry Santa hat to complete her outfit. "I'll only be outside for a few minutes, and after that, I guarantee that Bill will be keeping me toasty warm the rest of the night."

"Braggart," muttered Anna Marie.

"Why do you always think I can't hear you?"

"Why do you always think I don't want you to hear me?" retorted Anna Marie.

On the short drive to Bill's house, she popped a holiday music CD into the car player and turned the volume up. It was a great time of year, and she loved singing the familiar carols. By the time they arrived, Anna Marie was almost ready to concede that Sylvia's plan was a wonderfully romantic gesture.

As soon as the car came to a stop, Sylvia hopped out and scurried toward the porch. A light dusting of snow covered the walkway, and she had to be careful how she placed her feet. "Thank you!" she called out, waving her free hand as she shivered in the chill. "I'll call you tomorrow!"

Anna Marie just shook her head and smiled. Sylvia's exploits could fill a large book. Her *successful* exploits would fill a significantly smaller volume. She tooted the horn as she drove away and conceded she might actually need a little more of Syl's holiday attitude. She'd heard the local theater was playing the original "Miracle on 34th Street," and decided to go check it out.

Meanwhile, Sylvia struggled to pull the fleece stocking up around her bare shoulders. It wasn't quite long enough, even when she hunched down a little. *Damn,* she thought, *it's a lot colder than I imagined it would be.* She comforted herself by the fact that it was already quarter after five. Bill would be home in a matter of minutes. She smiled when she pictured the look on his face.

At 5:45 Sylvia's teeth began to chatter.

Across town, Bill decided to have the jewelry store clerk wrap the gift he had finally selected. He was sure Syl would love the necklace, but he didn't have the time, or the necessary skill, to go home and wrap it himself. He wanted to surprise her with it under the mistletoe at her place tonight.

"You know," said the clerk, "you just made it under the wire. We were going to close early, on account of it being Christmas Eve and we want to get home and all."

Bill smiled sheepishly. "What can I say?" He grinned. "I'm a guy."

"Poor excuse," admonished the female clerk.

"Only excuse I've got," laughed Bill. He nodded his head toward a half dozen other male shoppers still agonizing over the jewelry display cases. "And apparently I'm not the only one." He was feeling lighthearted and joyful and would have burst into song if there'd been any music playing.

He left the store with his small, precious package and decided on the spur of the moment to make an additional quick stop for a bottle of champagne. Sylvia loved champagne. And Bill particularly liked the way she giggled when the bubbles tickled her nose.

By the time he made his wine selection, it was a little after six. Instead of going home to shower and change, as originally planned, he drove straight to Syl's house. Her car was in the driveway, but no lights were on. He knocked on the front door. No answer. He dialed her cell phone and heard it ring inside the house. He went around the back of the house and found the key she left there "for emergencies."

Bill entered the back door and hurried through the house, flipping on all the lights and calling her name. He located her cell phone sitting on the credenza next to her purse. *Where was Syl if her purse was here?* Bill's heart pounded in his chest.

Sylvia was now huddled in a ball on Bill's porch, the stocking pulled completely over her head. She breathed on her hands and rubbed them vigorously on her legs, trying to warm them but careful not to put a run in her black sheer stockings. Shivering uncontrollably, she wondered what time it was, and chastised herself for leaving her phone behind.

Peering out from the top of the stocking, Sylvia could see the porch light on at a neighboring house a few hundred yards down the road. She weighed the pros and cons of abandoning her wrap and making a dash for it in her skimpy costume. She could live through the humiliation, but since she could not honestly tell if anyone was home, she decided to stay put. She couldn't imagine dashing to the neighboring house and back in her red high heels.

Bill sat down to think. *Should he call the police?* No. He'd call her best friend first. He picked up Syl's phone and saw Anna Marie's number was the last one called. He pressed the button, and heard it go straight to voice mail.

Now what? He paced for a few more minutes before it dawned on him that Syl and Anna Marie might be somewhere together. That would explain Syl's car being at home, *but her purse?*

Don't panic, he told himself. Don't panic. He dialed his home phone number to check his messages. Nothing. Bill pulled the gift box from his jacket pocket and eyed it lovingly. "Where are you, Syl?" he whispered.

At 6:30 Bill decided he'd be better off waiting at home. He pulled into his driveway just in time to see something resembling a giant red and white sleeping bag all tangled up and rolling in the snow across his lawn. He quickly parked the car, climbed out, and cautiously approached it.

Syl's nearly blue nose emerged from the top of the sock. *"Help,"* she whimpered.

Bill restrained himself from making a comment about how she'd fallen and couldn't get up. He also wisely fought back any trace of laughter. "Is there room in there for us both," he asked her with a straight face, "or would you like to come inside?"

Without waiting for a response, he gathered her up, bag and all, and carried her toward the house. He had a feeling it was going to take a little more than a bottle of champagne to get her warm again.

Sylvia put her arms around his neck. "M-M-M-Merry Chr-Chri-Christmas B-B-Bill…."

Bill gently kissed the top of her head. "Merry Christmas, my little snow bunny."

Love as a Souvenir

Marie couldn't wait. The moment she stepped through the heavy glass double sliding doors and walked into the air-conditioned lobby, she kicked off her shoes. She glanced at the clerk behind the reservation desk, but he was rapidly typing on a computer keyboard, so she tucked her sling-backs under her arm and started through the foyer. The cool red tile soothed her tired feet, and her spirits began to lift.

As she strode by the make-do bar nestled along one side of the wide hallway, Marie hesitated. The bartender, a young but balding man with dark-rimmed glasses, had no customers. He sat staring up at the muted Monday night football game projected on the small TV screen nestled between the bottles on display.

Marie edged closer, enough to see the game score, smiled, and impulsively climbed up on a leather-padded barstool directly in front of the television.

"What'll it be?" asked the bartender, suddenly coming to attention.

"Club soda with just a splash of cranberry juice, please."

He raised an eyebrow. "Had enough tonight?"

Marie shrugged, sighed, and recognized a familiar trace of annoyance at having to constantly explain her beverage choice. "I don't drink."

He poured her order, added a twist of lime to it, and set the sparkling glass on the bar in front of her. "May I have your autograph?" he inquired with a small smile.

Marie almost choked on her first sip. "My autograph?" she echoed.

"Yes," he replied, "I've been working here for eight years, and I've never met anyone who visited the French Quarter of New Orleans who didn't drink."

Marie rolled her hazel eyes and shook her head, making her long, wavy brown hair sway gently back and forth. "May I remind you," she said, "that you work in a bar?"

The bartender laughed. "Well, you got me on that one." He glanced back at the television. "You a football fan?"

"I'm from Seattle," said Marie, "and right now it looks like the Seahawks are going to clobber the 49ers, so I guess you could call me a fan tonight. When we're winning," she smiled, "it's easy to be a fan." She took another sip of her drink. "You could even turn the sound on, if you'd like."

The bartender scanned the empty hallway, rattan chairs and tables strategically scattered to give the illusion of a real lounge. "Well," he said, picking up the remote, "since it's just us."

They sat in companionable silence for a few minutes, engrossed in the game. Seattle scored for a third time, and both Marie and her server cheered enthusiastically.

"Mind if I sit down?" The low voice, so close to Marie's ear, startled her. She swiveled abruptly from the screen and was startled a second time when she came face to face with the most handsome man she'd ever seen. Her shoes and purse tumbled from her lap and scattered on the floor.

The olive-skinned man bent to retrieve her belongings while Marie restrained herself from reaching down to touch his wavy black hair. What a hunk. She scrambled to regain some semblance of composure.

"Thank you," was all she managed to say when he handed her shoes and purse back to her. "And yes, please, have a seat." She motioned to the barstool next to her.

The man grinned, revealing a set of beautiful white teeth, and bowed his head. "Grazie."

"John," he said, turning to the bartender, "what do you have on tap tonight?"

Marie waited quietly while the man placed his order, fumbling around in her mind for something witty and entertaining to say, and coming up blank.

The man took a tentative sip, nodded his approval, and turned once again to Marie. "Our server's name is on a placard above the cash register, next to the mirror," he said, anticipating her question. "But I am at a disadvantage when it comes to addressing you."

Marie thought she was speechless before, but this sealed it. She sat dumbstruck.

"I am Raphael," the man finally offered, breaking the awkward silence.

"Raphael," she repeated softly. And then, still desperate for something clever to say, blurted out, "like the Teenage Mutant Ninja Turtle?"

"I prefer," said Raphael, with just a touch of amusement in his tone, "that the name recalls to you an exceptional Italian Renaissance Artist."

Marie's face turned scarlet. "Of course," she murmured, quickly glancing back at the TV to avoid looking directly at him.

"However," Raphael continued matter-of-factly, "if that is too much of a stretch for you, you may call me Rafe." Marie scowled. Was he intentionally mocking her? She turned to face him and saw his teasing smile and twinkling dark brown eyes. At least half her wits returned. "Most people call me Marie," she said, extending her hand, "but my mother actually named me Maria, after Natalie Woods' character in West Side Story."

Raphael's smile deepened as he shook her hand. "Maria..." he whispered, his voice hinting at a subtle melody. "Maria. The most beautiful sound I've ever heard."

His knowledge of the 1961 classic scored big points with Maria. She felt a sudden easy camaraderie, and relaxed her guard. They chatted amicably for a time, discussing the unseasonably warm weather for November in New Orleans, the far-reaching effects, years later, of Hurricane Katrina, and whether crawfish or shrimp was preferable in authentic jambalaya.

Maria felt herself more and more drawn to this very sexy and highly intelligent man. She guessed they were about the same age—old enough to know better, but still young enough to want to do it. *Do it?!* She felt her face flush a second time at the unbidden thought.

Raphael, either not noticing her discomfort, or too much of a gentleman to mention it, returned his attention to the television monitor. "I must admit," he said, "I do not know as much about American football as American movies."

Maria welcomed the obvious segue. "When Seattle, which I fondly refer to as the land of my birth and the home of the Seahawks, has the most points on the board, it's a good thing. That's all you really need to know."

"Ah," replied Rafe, "then you are from the Pacific Northwest."

"Yes." Maria nodded. "I'm here on vacation, and I've got five days left. How about you?"

"I am currently working in the other Washington—Washington D.C., and I will be returning there tomorrow."

Tomorrow... Maria felt a sharp pang of disappointment. She stared at the small screen; there was nothing more to say.

John quietly refilled their glasses. He set a bowl of snack mix discreetly between them and retreated to his unobtrusive corner.

It took only a few minutes before Raphael reached into the munchies bowl. In doing so, his hand collided with Maria's. "Scusi," he said in his soft Italian accent.

"My fault," said Maria, abruptly pulling her hand away. "I shouldn't be so greedy."

"It is, I believe, only natural," said Rafe, looking directly into her eyes, "to want more of a good thing."

For a third time, Maria blushed, but this time she did not look away. "Yes," she said, "I can certainly agree with that."

John clicked off the TV, bringing Rafe and Maria out of their reverie. "Game's over," he said. "You two can sit here as long as you like, but I need to formally close the bar." He placed Rafe's tab on the counter. Motioning to Maria, he said, "No alcohol, no charge."

Raphael retrieved his wallet from his inside jacket pocket and paid his bill, including what Maria observed to be a healthy tip.

John closed out his till and locked the bottles behind sliding doors. "Have a good evening," he said as he took his jacket from a peg on the wall and exited through a side door into a back room.

Raphael cleared his throat. "Well," he said, "I guess it's probably time to call it a night."

"Yes," replied Maria, "I guess it is." She stood and used the back of the barstool to maintain her balance while she slipped back into her shoes.

"Maria—" Rafe began, then abruptly stopped and shook his head.

"Yes, Rafe?"

"I don't suppose…"

"You don't suppose what, Rafe?" Maria asked softly.

Decisively, Rafe extended his hand. "It was a pleasure meeting you, Maria."

"Nice meeting you, too," replied Maria. She felt the rush of excitement created by his handshake extend clear down to her toes. Impulsively, she reached into her purse and withdrew her business card. "Here," she said, handing it to him. "I work in an insurance office in Seattle. If you ever happen to get to Washington, the state, look me up."

"I will, Maria." Raphael tucked the card into his shirt pocket without even looking at it. "Sweet dreams."

Maria didn't trust herself to say anything else. She nodded and walked to the elevator while Rafe proceeded down the main hallway. Merely ships that pass in the night, she thought, and wondered if years from now she'd still be lamenting this missed opportunity to sail away into the sunset.

*   *   *

The next evening, when Maria arrived back in her room after a full day of sightseeing on the Mississippi River, the red message light on her phone was blinking.

Concerned that something might be amiss back home, she immediately accessed the voice mail.

"Maria," said the now-familiar and distinctly European voice, "I decided to extend my stay an extra day. I'd like to see you." The message had been left shortly after 9 a.m. It was now nearly 7 p.m.

"Damn!" she cursed aloud. "That's what I get for being such an early riser, even on vacation." Maria's heart was pounding as she called the desk. "Please," she said breathlessly, "please put me through to Raphael—" She stopped, suddenly realizing that she did not know his last name. "I'm sorry— There's this man—" Maria racked her brain, blurting out everything she could think of to track him down. "He's Italian— But he's from Washington D.C. — He left me a voice mail this morning— He was checking out today, but— I know he had a room on the first floor—"

"It's okay, honey," laughed the female desk clerk. "I know just who you mean. He did check out this morning, then about an hour later, he checked back in. I'll put you through to his new room."

Maria's heart raced into triple time. *What if he's not there?*

But he *was* there, picking up the receiver on the first ring. "Buon giorno"

"Rafe! You're still here!"

"Yes, Maria, I am still here. I have postponed my departure until 6 o'clock tomorrow morning."

"I'm so sorry. If I had only known you were going to stay another day–"

"Do not worry, Maria, I am here now." Raphael cleared his throat. "It is nearly seven," he said, "but the night is still young. Have you had dinner?"

"No," replied Maria. "I've had a full day of tourist

adventures, and hardly stopped to eat at all."

"Then you must be famished, as am I. If you would you care to join me for dinner, meet me in the lobby in 10 minutes."

"Ten minutes?!"

"I am sorry; do you need more time to… freshen up?"

"I'll be there in nine and a half," laughed Maria.

Rafe was already in the lobby when she exited the elevator. His eyes lit up when he saw her, and he moved forward, extending his hand. But instead of the handshake Maria expected, Raphael lifted her hand to his lips and brushed it gently with a soft kiss. Maria felt the goose bumps tingle both her arms and move rapidly up to the back of her neck. She took a deep, steadying breath.

"So nice to see you again," she managed to say.

"The pleasure is mine." He put a protective arm across her lower back as they left the hotel. Maria felt instantly warm and safe and cherished. For a time, she didn't even think to ask where they were going, and simply basked in this new feeling of belonging.

Maria stole a sidelong look at him as they walked. He was wearing gray slacks and a light blue long-sleeved shirt. There was nothing remarkable about his clothing, yet he looked sophisticated and professional. She was glad she had hastily changed from her Jamaican shorts and tank top into a green and gold knee-length sleeveless dress before joining him in the lobby.

Raphael finally broke the silence. "I discovered a very nice little Cajun restaurant not far from here. I hope you like Crawfish Etouffee."

"I don't know," replied Maria. "What is it?"

Rafe laughed. "It is essentially a plate of peeled

crawfish tails smothered in a stew of chopped onions, peppers, and garlic. But if you'd like something else, the menu has many offerings from which to choose."

They stopped at an intersection and Maria looked up at him. "I'll have the A-two-fay," she replied, attempting to duplicate his pronunciation. "I like to try new things." She tucked her hand into the crook of his arm while they waited for the light to change.

"Then you would not be averse to going to a quaint little blues club down on Bourbon Street after dinner?" Rafe inquired.

"How quaint?"

Raphael could not keep a straight face. "It's called the Funky Pirate."

"Perfect," said Maria, laughing delightedly. "The whole evening sounds perfect."

Their dinner, as expected, was superb. And it wasn't until they were approaching the club, hand-in-hand, that Maria thought to ask Raphael how he had happened to know how to get a message to her at the hotel.

"My dear Maria," he chuckled. "I am tempted to tell you I visited a psychic in Jackson Square at dawn this morning, or some such nonsense. Do you not remember that you handed me your business card as you left the lobby last night?"

"I didn't think you even looked at it."

"I must admit, I could see only you at the time, but I put it in the pocket closest to my heart to hold it near to me for later viewing."

"Has anyone ever told you," said Maria, shaking her head, "that sometimes you're just a tad bit schmoozy?"

"This schmoozy, is it a good thing?"

"Not usually," replied Maria, with a twinkle in her

eye, "but tonight it just might work for you."

They entered the bar, already packed with locals and tourists, and wrangled for two chairs to squeeze in at a table already occupied with several other people. The air was filled with jovial voices calling out to friends and trying to hold conversations by out-shouting the background music. Rafe's eyes followed Maria's to a sign above the bar proclaiming the Funky Pirate as the "Home of the Hand Grenade, the most powerful drink on Bourbon Street."

Raphael leaned in close to Maria's ear. "They also have a drink called the Hurricane, but I don't think it's an exclusive to the Tropical Isle."

Maria turned her head to whisper back in his proffered ear, "I'll pass." He shook his head, unable to make out her words. "I said, no thank you," she fairly shouted.

Rafe gave her a thumbs-up sign and went to the bar. He returned with a club soda and cranberry juice for her, and a beer for himself. Maria was impressed; he'd been paying attention the night before.

Since conversation was nearly impossible, Maria studied her surroundings with interest. The tropical motif included swashbuckling pirates, parrots, and plenty of palm trees and flowering greenery decorated the room. It was a bright, happy place, and Maria's heart was full to capacity with joy and possibility.

Then the house lights dimmed, and Big Al and The Blues Masters took the stage. Thunderous applause and numerous whistles, the kind that take two fingers stuck in your mouth to create, overshadowed the former noise in the crowded room. Big Al picked up the microphone to welcome the group.

"Wow," said Maria, directly into Rafe's ear again.

"He certainly lives up to his name." By her estimation, Big Al was on the far side of 500 pounds.

Raphael smiled. "With a big blues heart to match," he replied. Rafe had obviously been here before. Big Al crooned song after song, interspersed with humorous commentary and banter with the locals. His voice, even when just joking with the crowd, carried Maria off to her own land of fantasy and romance.

"Would you care to dance?" Rafe asked her early in the second set.

"Dance?" echoed Maria, as if she hadn't heard correctly. Could this night get any better? Unsteadily, she rose to her feet. Rafe took her hand, and they wound their way through the scattered tables to the dance floor. He turned, and gently pulled her into his arms. Maria thought her knees would give out in a total swoon.

He held her close, but not too close, swaying more from the torso up than attempting to move his feet in the jam-packed space before the bandstand. Maria wasn't sure her feet were touching the ground at all. One song led to another, and Maria lost track of reality as she floated in the softness of Raphael's embrace, her dress swirling softly about her as if in a beautiful dream.

When Big Al took a break, Rafe guided her out the double doors and onto the cobbled street for a breath of fresh air.

"Whew," said Maria, finally able to speak in a normal tone of voice. "I forget what it's like to be out in a bar that still allows smoking." She fanned her face with her hand. "And it was so hot in there!"

Rafe clucked his tongue. "And here I thought it was just the proximity of our bodies while we danced that had brought such color to your face."

Maria laughed. "Raphael, you're one smooth talker."

"I think that you shall find," said Raphael, leaning closer to her as he spoke, "that I am also a fine kisser." He softly cupped her face in his hands and lowered his lips to hers. Maria willingly met his advance, with a gentle longing and passion she had too long held in abeyance. She wrapped her arms around him and pulled him tight against her.

After their deep and lustful kiss, they parted breathless and stood uncertainly on the neon-lit street corner, both of them painfully aware of their present surroundings.

"You have an early plane," said Maria at last. She looked at her watch to avoid looking in his eyes. "And it is already quite late."

"Are you ready, then, to return to the hotel?" asked Rafe, tenderly tucking a strand of her long hair behind her left ear.

Maria resisted the urge to shiver as his touch, and considered the viable options for a moment. Since grabbing him by the shirtfront and planting another deep, passionate kiss on him seemed a bit too bold, she replied, "Yes, I think I am ready to leave, if you are."

"It has been a long day," replied Rafe. "And I am thinking it would be nice to sit and chat some more with you in the company of John, our favorite bartender. There, I am sure, we would be able to converse in more subdued voices."

But due to the lateness of the hour, John had already closed up shop before they arrived. "Never fear," said Raphael, offering her a chair with a gallant bow. "I will procure us some sodas from the machine in the hallway and we shall continue our discourse."

And talk they did. Although Maria protested at several junctures in their conversation that Rafe would soon be going directly to the airport without any sleep at all, he insisted he was fine, and that he could sleep on the plane.

Maria learned more about Raphael's native home in Italy, about his current government job, which is what had brought him to New Orleans in the first place, and of his three college-aged children. It had not occurred to Maria that Raphael might have adult offspring. Having had no children herself, she was always a little surprised to hear of friends her age becoming grandparents.

The dots finally connected in Maria's mind, and she grappled with a question she felt compelled to ask. "And what about your wife?" Maria blurted out, knowing instantly that she had phrased the question poorly.

"My wife?" asked a startled Raphael.

"Your children must have a mother."

Raphael quickly shook his head. "I do not like to talk about my wife."

Tears stung Maria's eyes as she sprang instantly to her feet. "I am sorry, Raphael," she began. "I— I must go to my room now." She turned and literally ran toward the elevator.

"Maria!"

But the elevator was already there, waiting for her. She stepped inside and hastily pressed the "close door" button. As the lift rose to her floor, Maria leaned against the wall and sobbed, her heart breaking into more pieces than she'd even known it had.

*   *   *

94

Maria awoke to bright sunlight streaming in her window. Remembering that she had not returned to the room until the wee hours of the morning, she was still surprised to realize she had slept so long. She rolled over to look at the digital clock on the nightstand. "Nine-thirty!" she said aloud, and was suddenly overcome by waves of sadness as she recalled the events of the previous night. She sat up and glared at the phone. There was no message light blinking. *Just as well.*

She showered, dressed in the same Jamaicas and tank top she had worn the day before, and hurried down to the breakfast room. Selecting a banana muffin, some orange juice and a cup of decaf coffee, Maria picked up a copy of the local newspaper and headed for a table at the far end of the room. More than anything else, she just wanted to be left alone. But the hotel staff had other ideas.

"Miss? Excuse me, Miss? Is your name Maria?"

Maria turned to see the morning reservation clerk hurrying her way. The clerk handed her a folded-over piece of paper. "A gentleman left this for you very early this morning. He said he didn't want to disturb you before he checked out, but to make sure you got it right away."

Maria thanked the woman and placed the note on the table before her. Absently, she picked at the walnuts in her muffin and sipped her coffee. She tried to focus on the morning news show, but to no avail. She opened the newspaper and flipped through it distractedly. Finally, just to put an end to her angst, she picked up the note, and without reading it, wadded it up tightly in her hand.

No, she thought, *I most certainly will not get involved with a married man.* She gathered what was left of her breakfast and dumped the trash, along with the note, into the receptacle next to the door on her way out.

Not needing to return to her room for anything, Maria left the hotel through the main entrance. There she hesitated. To the right a few blocks was the restaurant where she and Rafe had eaten their cozy little dinner the night before. To the left was Bourbon Street, where she felt certain they had created an intimate connection while they danced.

Maria shook her head to clear the memories. She thought about hopping on the St. Charles streetcar and riding it to the end of the line, wherever that might be. But she opted instead to angle off down a side street toward the banks of the Mississippi River. The sun was already making little heat waves rise from the pavement, and she was grateful to find several empty benches in the park near the steamboat landing. Overhanging trees provided ample shade, and a gentle breeze was playing off the water.

She sat in her own little stupor, only peripherally aware of the coming and going of the steamboats Natchez and Creole Queen, and paid no attention at all to the single white egret that magically appeared on the banks of the river only a few feet before her. Under normal circumstances, Marie would have been enchanted by her surroundings, and enthralled by the appearance of the egret. But today she just sat and mulled over the events of the past two days.

The remainder of her vacation was predominantly consumed by sitting on park benches, either along the river or in Jackson Square, pondering the choices she had made in the course of her life. Her fiftieth birthday was behind her; it had been over 20 years since her short marriage and subsequent divorce. She'd thrown herself into her work back then, and had rarely surfaced long enough to date more than a few times.

Sometimes Maria thought there must be something wrong with her, and sometimes she thought she was better off without all the pain that seemed to accompany most of her friends' relationships. But still she longed for that magical connection. She wanted to be loved and treasured and cherished and revered. She wanted to be the most important thing in someone's life. She yearned to see the man she loved walk into a room and feel her heart skip with joy. As silly as it sounded, she wanted to feel her toes curl when the man she loved kissed her.

But Maria worried now that it was much too late for her, and that such a deep, abiding, romantic love only existed in the movies. *Would she ever get her turn?*

*   *   *

It was almost a relief to return to work at the insurance office the following Monday. Her co-workers greeted her enthusiastically, telling her she looked wonderfully rested and how envious they were that she had had such great weather to enjoy in The Big Easy. To each she smiled, nodded, and agreed that the weather had been marvelous. To each she handed a string of souvenir purple and green Mardi Gras beads, and proceeded through the room without being held too long in any one spot by personal conversation.

"Marie!" exclaimed Sharon, her best friend and office mentor, jumping up to give her a hearty hug as soon as she hung up her coat on the rack between their cubicles. "Dish, girlfriend! I want to hear all about it!"

Marie shook her head. "Not much to tell." She flipped on her computer and looked abstractedly at the stack of phone messages piled on her desk.

"Not much to tell?" asked Sharon, raising an eyebrow. "Well then, my dear friend, who is obviously withholding vital information, just who, exactly, is Raphael?"

Marie froze. She opened her mouth, but no sound came out. She closed her mouth, cleared her throat, tried again to find her voice, but failed a second time.

"Nice guppy imitation," giggled Sharon. "You look just like the fish in my aquarium." She squinted her eyes at Marie, and using a rather poor German accent, said, "But ve have vays to make you talk…"

"Raphael," Marie whispered, almost inaudibly. "How do you know about Raphael?"

"Geez, Mare," said Sharon, "I answer your phone while you're gone, remember? Over half those messages are from the same guy. What'd you do in New Orleans, anyway? Leave some poor schmuck heartbroken?"

Marie quickly sorted though the little pink slips. "Call me." "Let me explain." "It's not what you think." "Please give me a chance." She looked up at Sharon, who stood patiently waiting for a reply. "Nothing happened in New Orleans," she said, and threw the messages from Rafe into the bin marked for the shredder.

Sharon clicked her tongue and shook her head, but said nothing. She walked a few steps to her own workstation and sat down. "Let me know if you want to talk about it," she said over her shoulder.

When Marie accessed her email, she discovered over two hundred entries had found their way to her inbox in the week she'd been gone. She scanned the list and sighed. "I thought our new security system was supposed to filter out the junk mail," she said to Sharon. "I've got more than 20 messages from some lousy spammer.

"That's odd," replied Sharon. "I haven't gotten any spam in months." She approached Marie's desk and peered over her shoulder. "Hhmmm…. The server it comes from looks legit," she said. "Why don't you open the one of them and check it out?"

"Because this is my business email," replied Marie, "and I don't know anyone who uses the name 'RenaissanceMan', that's why." She began repeatedly hitting the delete key. "Besides, all the subject lines just say 'Please read' and no real subject is indicated. Probably a porn spammer or one of those Viagra-by-mail offers."

"Well, you're not going to know for sure unless you open one of them," said Sharon. "You can't get a virus unless you open an attachment, you know. Regular emails won't hurt you."

"Too late," said Marie, pressing the delete key a final time. "All gone bye-bye."

She spent the rest of the morning hunched over her desk, attacking her backlog of files and accounts with a vengeance. By noon, she felt some sense of control over the work left to do and eagerly accepted an invitation to go to lunch with Sharon, but with one condition: "We're not going to talk about New Orleans."

After lunch Marie was dismayed to find five more emails from RenaissanceMan. "How do you permanently block a spam site?" she asked Sharon.

Sharon scooted her chair over to Marie's desk and took the computer mouse in her own hand. "Here, I'll show you—" Then she stopped. "The most recent one is different," she continued, puzzled. "The subject line is in all caps. It says 'I'm a widower.'" And without waiting for Marie's approval, Sharon impulsively clicked open the email message. "What's this—?"

"Oh my God—" Tears sprang to Marie's eyes as she read the two-line message. "My wife died three years ago. Please let me hear from you. Raphael."

The women sat speechless. Finally Sharon put her hand on Marie's arm, expelled a long breath, and said, "Girlfriend, I think you'll want to answer this one."

"I guess so," replied Marie after a lengthy pause. "I'm afraid I've made a terrible mistake."

" It's probably nothing that can't be fixed," said Sharon. "But you'll never know unless you try." She shuffled her chair back into her own space and left Marie to sort it out for herself.

It was past five o'clock by the time Marie the courage to press the reply button on Rafe's email. Now what? She sat and stared at the blinking cursor. The words didn't come. Sharon was gathering her coat and purse and preparing to head for home.

"Need some help?" she asked her friend. "I'll stay for moral support if you need me."

"What I need," said Marie, "is someone to ghost write this email."

"Just speak from your heart," said Sharon. "Just write what you'd say if you were talking to him."

"You mean something like, 'I'm an idiot'?"

"No, I mean something a little less self-deprecating. Don't put yourself down. You obviously had no idea."

"That's good," said Marie, and she began to type: "Dear Rafe, I had no idea..." and then her fingers stalled. She looked up imploringly at Sharon, who stood poised to leave. "And *then* what do I say?"

Sharon just shook her head. "You're on your own, baby cakes. See you in the morning. Good night, and good luck." She gave Marie's shoulder as squeeze as she walked by. "You can do this."

Marie sat still for a few more minutes, then she decided the best thing to do was to abandon the whole darn thing for the time being. *I'll sleep on it. I'll know what to write in the morning. I just need some time to think about it. There's no rush.* She quickly moved the mouse to press the 'close' box, but in her haste pressed the 'send' button instead... "Oh my God," she said for the second time that day.

*   *   *

"If you don't mind me saying so," said Sharon the next morning, "you don't look so good."

"Thanks a lot," replied Marie. "It's always nice for people to notice how rotten you feel."

"Didn't you sleep, honey?"

"Hardly a wink." Marie explained the cause of her sleeplessness to a compassionate Sharon while they walked to the break room for coffee. "Today I'm foregoing the decaf for a strong jolt of caffeine."

Returning to her cubicle, she flipped on her computer. "Hold my hand, Sharon." Sharon raised both eyebrows. "I mean that metaphorically," clarified Marie. Her email appeared and she scanned the incoming list. "No response." She bit her lower lip and tried to keep her voice steady. "I don't blame him."

It's just another Tuesday, she told herself. *Just another fun-filled day at the insurance office.* She vowed to throw herself into every claim form, every request for review, every possible focus for her wandering attention to help keep her mind from thinking too much.

Shortly before noon, Marie's concentration was broken by the sound of Sharon exclaiming, "Oh wow! Would you look at that!"

She raised her head and turned in the direction Sharon pointed. A young man was carrying an enormous floral arrangement through the office, and he was headed their way. Marie thought her face would burst into flames when he set the enormous vase full of roses on her desk and handed her the accompanying card. She sat totally dumbstruck.

Sharon handed the young man a tip and thanked him, then turned to her friend. "Well," she said, "are you just going to sit there, or are you going to open it?"

Marie examined the envelope in her hand. "Maria." She felt a brick lodge itself in her throat as she carefully opened it and slipped the card out. "The most beautiful sound I've ever heard."

Through watering eyes, she looked up at Sharon. "They're from Raphael," she said huskily.

"And they're thornless," said Sharon. "You know what that means?"

Marie shook her head.

"Thornless roses signify love at first sight."

Marie said nothing. She alternately stared at the card in her hand, then at the roses, then back at the card, then back to the roses. While her mind raced in a million different directions, she sat completely transfixed, unable to form words or take action.

"So," said Sharon to break the silence, "the next question is, you gonna sit there all day with that goofy look on your face, or you going to go lunch with me?"

Marie smiled up at her friend. "Lunch sounds good," she said. "And then I believe I have a very important thank you note to write."

But more work was piled high on her desk when they returned from lunch, and Marie had to postpone writing Raphael for a few hours. It was approaching five o'clock by the time she could turn her full attention to drafting a heartfelt thank you. She gazed at the roses for a long time, softly smiling, and pressed "compose" to create a new email.

"Ahem..." Sharon tried to draw Marie's attention by exaggeratedly clearing her throat. "Ahem... Marie..." she stage-whispered.

Deep into her thoughts, Marie barely acknowledged her friend. "Hhhmmm... What?" she asked distractedly.

"Marie—" Sharon's voice was more urgent now. "Marie, I don't think you ought to bother finishing that email."

Marie's head popped up. "What are you talking about?"

Sharon nodded towards the doorway. Marie looked in the direction she motioned.

A dark-haired, well-groomed man of obvious Mediterranean descent stood at the entrance, craning his neck to see above the cubicles as he searched the room with his eyes. The security guard at the door pointed in her direction.

Marie gasped. "Raphael," she whispered.

It was impossible for him to have heard her, yet suddenly he was moving rapidly in her direction, calling out to her as he wove his way through the workstations. "Maria! Maria!"

She stood trembling as he approached, one hand holding onto the edge of the desk for balance. He stopped a few feet in front her, suddenly at a loss for words.

Maria swallowed hard and indicated the flowers on her desk with her free hand. "The flowers," she said, "are lovely."

"Not nearly as lovely as the woman I sent them to," began Raphael. His smile was warm and genuine and wrinkled the corners of his eyes. "You are even more lovely than I remember."

Maria shook her head and tried, unsuccessfully, to communicate that she wasn't buying his smooth talking by doing an eye roll. "Rafe, we just met last week."

"Ah, then it is a week we have wasted apart," he said in his thick accent. He got down on one knee, and took her hands in his.

"Rafe, what are you doing?" asked an incredulous Maria, looking around to discover all of her colleagues shamelessly watching the spectacle. She lowered her voice. "Rafe, get up, you're embarrassing me."

"Maria," continued Raphael, even louder, "Maria, I want the whole world to know how much I love you. Marry me, Maria."

Although Maria's knees were in danger of buckling right out from under her, this time she did not quite lose her ability to speak. "Marry you?"

"Say 'yes,' Maria."

Her co-workers, unused to any type of excitement or distraction during office hours, quickly took up the chant, "Say yes! Say yes! Say yes!"

She held up her hand to silence them. "Raphael," she said, "I haven't stopped thinking about you since the moment we met. I believe when two people are destined to be together, love will find a way. When I gave you my business card, I had no idea how that one small gesture would change my life, but it did." She paused for breath.

"Marie— MARIA…" interjected Sharon, eager to help her friend. "Enough with the speeches, already. You've got the man on his knees, for crying out loud!"

Maria laughed at Sharon's impatience, then turned her full attention back to Raphael. "Yes, Rafe." She bent and kissed his forehead. "Yes, yes, yes, yes yes!"

Raphael sprung quickly to his feet and embraced her, to the cheering and applause of the entire office staff. "You shall all be invited to the wedding!" he called out, before he kissed her with such fervor that she could truly feel her toes curl.

"Next year," said Sharon to no one in particular as she returned to her desk, "next year I think I just might take *my* vacation in New Orleans!"

Love Comes Knocking

"Who is it?" Shelly called out.

"Cable repairman," replied the man standing on the other side of the closed door. "I've come to install your television service."

Shelly froze with her hand on the doorknob. *Cable repair?* How did she know the voice was that of a legitimate service technician? "Do you have some identification?"

"Yes, I sure do," responded the voice. "But since there's no peephole in your door, you're going to have to open up to see it."

Peephole, thought Shelly. *I'll have to put "peephole" at the top of my to-do list.* But that wouldn't solve her immediate problem.

"I have an idea," said the man, responding to her silence. "Look out your front window."

Bewildered, Shelly peered out the window of her fourth story apartment. Parked on the street below was a very large and well-marked cable company bucket truck. She smiled, and returned to the door, opening it just a crack.

"I still need to see some photo ID," she said unnecessarily as the man immediately offered his company identification to her. Shelly closed the door again while she examined the card.

Allan Freele, Coast Communications. The man in

the picture looked like he was probably somewhere in his mid-forties, like Shelly. He had a sharply receding hairline, wire-rimmed glasses, and a very nice smile. She opened the door, wider this time, and was rewarded with the same warm smile as in the photo.

"Please come in." Shelly stepped back to allow him to enter. "And please excuse the mess. I'm just moving in." *What a dumb thing to say!* she chastised herself. *Of course you're just moving in, that's why you called for cable installation!* She felt her cheeks grow warm as she pointed out where she wanted the outlets placed.

As he carried his equipment from room to room, Allan couldn't help but notice how attractive Shelly was. Her short, curly brown hair flatteringly framed a heart-shaped face. Attractive, smart, and single, he surmised, noting that the installation order was in her name only.

Allan chatted as he worked, telling Shelly how much she was going to like living here, where the post office was located, and which restaurants served the best seafood.

While they exchanged polite conversation, Shelly found herself appreciating the way the corners of Allan's eyes crinkled when he laughed, and the fact that he wore no wedding ring. *Which doesn't mean a thing these days,* she reminded herself.

Soon Shelly felt totally at ease with Allan and was sorry he worked so quickly. "I'd offer you a cup of coffee if I knew which box the coffeemaker was in," she said as he gathered up his tools.

"I'll take a rain check," Allan replied. "But thanks for the offer." He turned and headed for the door. "Your installation fee will be included on your first month's bill. Have a nice day."

Have a nice day, thought Shelly as she watched the

truck pull away from the curb. *Have a nice day.* Here she'd been thinking there might be a mutual connection developing, and all he said when he left was "Have a nice day."

Shelly sighed, and returned to the daunting task of unpacking. The coffeemaker was in the bottom of the very first box. "A lot of good you are!" she said aloud as she set it on the kitchen counter with a resounding thud.

Weeks later, Shelly found herself straining to catch a glimpse of the driver in each cable bucket truck she passed on the road between her apartment and her office. *So what if you happen to see him?* she asked herself a dozen times. *Are you going to flag him down to say hello? Not likely.* But still Shelly hoped she hadn't seen the last of Allan Freele's terrific smile.

When her first cable bill arrived, she tossed it on the dining room table along with all her other bills. Payday wasn't until next week, so she was in no hurry to open any of them.

Early Friday evening Shelly was contemplating what to fix for dinner, when a knock sounded at her door. "Who is it?" she called out.

"Cable repairman," came the reply.

"There's nothing wrong with my cable," she answered. "I didn't call for any service."

"I know," the voice answered, "that's why I wrote you the note."

Note? Shelly glanced at the cable bill's envelope on the table. Hastily, she ripped it open. Scrawled across the top of the bill someone had written "Have you found your coffeemaker yet? I'm ready to claim that rain check."

"Allan?" she asked.

"How many cable guys have you offered coffee to

since you moved in?"

Shelly laughed as she swung the door open. "Counting you, only one."

"Well that's a relief," replied Allan, rewarding her with another one of his genuine smiles, "cause I saw you first." He stepped inside. "But I have a confession to make."

Uh-oh, thought Shelly. She didn't like that way that sounded. "A confession?"

"Yes, of sorts." Allan cleared his throat. "You see, I don't actually drink coffee." From behind his back he produced a big bouquet of flowers. "So I'm here on false pretenses."

Shelly felt her face flush in his presence for the second time as she accepted the bouquet. "That's actually a good thing," she said as Allan followed her to the kitchen. She pulled the carafe from the coffeemaker and filled it with water. "Since I didn't bring any vases with me when I moved, I'm going to have to use this instead."

Now it was Allan's turn to laugh. As he helped her arrange the flowers, he said, "Now I know what to bring you the next time I come over."

"You don't like my vase?" Shelly asked coyly. Inside her head she was celebrating the fact that he'd indicated a "next time."

"Nope. Not a vase, a peephole. And I'll install it for you, too."

"I don't know," replied Shelly with a smile. "I think I'd have to see some more ID before I'd let you do a thing like that."

"No problem," said Allan. "My company truck is parked right outside."

"That may have worked once—" she began, shaking her head. "But do you have any peephole installation references?"

Allan laughed again. "All this talk about work has given me one voracious appetite," he teased. "How about I take you to dinner where you can interview me to your heart's content?"

"My heart's content?" Shelly exaggeratingly batted her eyelashes. Her heart already felt as content as it had ever been.

Making a Connection

Karen unzipped her laptop carrying case, extracted its contents and set her computer gently down on the only remaining table in the back room of the coffee shop. This was getting to be a very popular place, now that they offered free Wi-Fi service.

She took off her coat, draped it over the back of the accompanying chair, and went into the adjoining room to order her nonfat, decaf, grandé latte with a shot of sugar-free hazelnut flavoring. She smiled as she dug into her wallet. Life had sure been easier back when ordering a cup of coffee wasn't quite so complicated.

"We'll bring it right out to you," said one of the young women running the machines behind the counter.

"Thank you," said Karen, dropping the change into the tip jar next to the cash register. Three dollars for a cup of coffee, she mused. Well, at least here she got to use the Internet for free.

She went back through the archway and stopped abruptly. Someone had moved her coat and her laptop, and they were now in a pile on the couch. An unshaven and disheveled-looking man was sitting in her place typing furiously on his own keyboard. She rushed right up to the offender and tapped him on the shoulder.

"Excuse me," she said, feeling both righteous and indignant.

"Give me a few minutes," said the man without looking up. "I don't like to be interrupted when I'm in the middle of a thought."

Karen felt her face growing red. "And I don't like being ignored when I'm trying to talk to you." She stood her ground. The man continued to type. The all-too-perky cashier came in to hand Karen her drink.

"Is this a friend of yours?" the woman asked, nodding toward the man at the table.

"Not likely," said Karen through gritted teeth. She took the coffee from the woman, who hastily retreated. Karen made no move to abandon her position.

The man finally stopped typing and looked up. "Yes?" he said.

"You're in my seat," said Karen.

"There was no one here when I came in," said the man.

"No one here?!" asked an incredulous Karen. "My laptop was on the table, my coat was on the chair, and you say there was no one here?"

"Right," said the man. "And now, if you'll excuse me, I have work to do."

Karen considered dumping her latte in his lap. "No," she said, "I will not excuse you, or your bad manners. This is my table, and I also need to get some work done."

"Look," said the man, "possession is nine-tenths of the law."

"And I suppose you're an attorney?"

"All I'm saying is, you could sit somewhere else. You can connect to this Wi-Fi from your car in the parking lot if you wanted to."

"You think I should go out and sit in my car in front of the coffee shop to do my work?"

"You could."

"No, I couldn't," said Karen. "I need the wall outlet to plug it in. My battery won't hold a charge."

"Well, I need the outlet for the same reason, and I was here first."

Uncharacteristically, Karen refused to be bullied. She simply bent down and unplugged the man's laptop.

"Hey!" he yelled. "Just what do you think you're doing?"

Noting the volume and tone of his voice, the cashier came scurrying back in. "What seems to be the problem?" she asked.

The man took the cord from Karen's outstretched hand, snapped his laptop closed, and said to the cashier, "No problem." He glared at Karen. "You're costing me both time and money," he said, preparing to leave.

The cashier looked at Karen, who shrugged. "He was just leaving," she said, moving her coat and laptop to take the seat now vacated. She was grateful the other patrons of the shop were pretending to be busily minding their own business as she settled right down to her work.

The next morning Karen approached the coffee shop with some trepidation. During the course of the previous evening she had suffered pangs of remorse for her earlier behavior. She tried to rationalize that rudeness begets rudeness, but she knew she'd been raised better than that.

Thankfully, the coffee shop had plenty of spaces available, and she chose to take a position at a different table altogether. She plugged in her laptop and immersed herself in Internet research.

"Excuse me," said a pleasant male voice a half an hour later. "I think you're in my seat."

Startled, Karen looked up to into the face of yesterday's surly antagonist beaming at her. He had shaved, combed his hair, and didn't look like quite such a bully today.

"I'm glad you're here," he said. "I brought this for you." He handed her a purple hyacinth in a pot wrapped with lavender foil. "I behaved poorly yesterday. I was on deadline, but it's no excuse."

His words tumbled out in a rush. "The purple hyacinth is supposed to mean 'I'm sorry; please forgive me.' I looked it up on the Internet."

Karen smiled, accepted the flowering plant, and mentally chastised herself for taking note of the fact that he wore no wedding ring. "Thank you… Mr…. ?"

"Greg. My name's Greg," he said, nodding to her. "And I also brought this." He reached into his backpack and extracted a small multi-outlet power strip. He glanced around the room. "But I see it's not so busy here today." He sounded disappointed.

"We can still share a table," said Karen, scooting her chair over, "if you'll let *me* apologize by buying you a cup of coffee."

"It's a deal," Greg replied.

Rooting for the Home Team

"Run Mark, run!" Janice yelled from the top row of the bleachers.

"He's out!" bellowed the umpire, jerking his right thumb high into the air.

"He was safe by a mile!" Janice hollered back.

The man seated on the bleacher directly in front of her turned his head and smiled. "I take it that's your son?"

Janice blushed. "I'm sorry—I was yelling right into your ear, wasn't I?" She couldn't help but notice the warmth of his smile and his soft hazel eyes. "I don't believe we've met. Do you have a child on this team?"

"Sure do." He extended his hand. "And my name's Landon, Landon Jeffers."

"Janice Andrews."

It must be the chilly air combined with the material in the clothing she wore, decided Janice. What she felt was static electricity, nothing more. But she smiled to herself, happy to discover she was still the eternal romantic optimist.

Automatically, her eyes scanned the seats on either side of Landon. No visible wife, and he wore no wedding ring—although that rarely meant anything these days.

Focusing back on the game, Janice clapped and yelled enthusiastically as one of Mark's teammates hit the ball. Unfortunately, the runner was called out at first base.

"That's ok!" she encouraged the player, "You'll get 'em next time!"

Landon turned once again. Janice observed the way his dark hair was fringed with gray where it curled behind his ears. "Would you mind if I joined you up there?" he inquired with a sparkle in his eye. "I have a feeling it'd be a whole lot easier on my eardrums."

Janice's blush deepened. "Of course." She moved her thermos bottle to the other side of her feet and rearranged the plaid blanket beneath her. "Have a seat." She patted the space next to her. "The blanket's a lot warmer than sitting on bare wood."

"Thanks." Landon stood and stepped over his previous seat to the row above and settled himself on the bench beside her. "I'd forgotten how hard and cold these bleachers can feel on one's behind."

"Would you like a cup of coffee? It'll warm you up."

"I most certainly would, thanks." He took the Styrofoam cup she offered. "Are you always so well-organized?"

"Heaven's no!" laughed Janice. "The first game I brought the cups and left the thermos sitting on the kitchen counter. The second game I didn't remember the blanket, and last week—"

"Don't leave me hanging." Landon smiled his encouragement. He liked the way her naturally rosy cheeks deepened as she told on herself. "Please, tell me, what happened last week?"

Janice shook her head but continued. "Last week we searched all over the house for Mark's uniform. We totally turned the place inside out. We looked in every drawer, every closet, under every bed, even in the dog's bed!" She laughed and paused to take a sip of coffee.

"You must have found it," interjected Landon, "unless that's a new uniform he's wearing today."

"We found it all right," said Janice. "In the nick of time, I suddenly thought to look in the dryer." She winced at the memory. "What kind of mother leaves clothes to wrinkle in the dryer for a week? By then, we were almost late for the game." She grinned sheepishly. "I hope I can get it all together by the end of the season!"

Landon joined her in good-natured laughter. Here was a down-to-earth woman who wasn't afraid to admit she wasn't perfect. He thought about that for a moment before he said softly, "I'm afraid this is the first chance I've had to come to a game." He sighed, then chuckled. "And here I show up without cushion, coffee or cups!"

"You'll be more prepared next time."

Landon sighed again. "Barbara's the one who effortlessly manages all those pesky little details."

Janice's smile froze on her lips. She hoped her voice sounded somewhat natural and disinterested when she asked, "Barbara's your wife?"

"Ex-wife." Landon shrugged. "I guess that makes me one of those 'weekend dads'."

Janice released her breath. Her eyes met his. "But today's Tuesday."

"I rearranged my work schedule to be here— Barbara's new husband had a business dinner she had to attend with him, so she asked me to cover for her. I've been meaning to come to some of the games anyway, but, well, I guess since the divorce two years ago I've spent most of my so-called free time hunched over my desk at work."

Janice looked at him out of the corner of her eye. "Then you think you'll be attending more often?"

"You can count on it." Dimples accompanied his

dazzling smile.

They sat for a while in companionable silence. Soon their team took the field. Janice felt the pride as Mark, number 34, took his position at third base. A player in jersey number 32 with "Jeffers" printed across the back trotting out to second. "What's your son's name?"

"Elizabeth."

Janice's face grew red one more time. "Oops…"

"It's okay," said Landon, touching her arm compassionately. "Lizzie keeps her hair pretty short—"

His words were cut off as the bat cracked. A base hit! The runner streaked around first and headed for second trying to turn it into a double. Although the ball had gone over Mark's head, he beat the left fielder to it and made a strong throw to second. Lizzie made a great catch and tagged the runner before his foot touched the base.

Landon and Janice had both jumped to their feet. "He's out!" they shouted in unison.

In her excitement, Janice bounced a little too hard on the wooden slats beneath her feet, knocked over the thermos, and momentarily lost her balance. Landon instinctively grabbed her hand to steady her. He was still holding it as they resettled themselves on the bleachers.

"Looks like our kids make a pretty good team," said Landon thoughtfully. "And, if I'm not being too forward, we might make a pretty good team ourselves."

Janice smiled, but kept her eyes on the game. She didn't dare look at him for fear she might be dreaming.

"So how 'bout we take the kids for ice cream after the game?" he asked a few minutes later.

"Win or lose?" asked Janice.

"I think," replied Landon, squeezing her hand, "we may have already won."

For the Love of Goldfish

Shelia stared into the store's goldfish tank and sighed. All the fish looked alike to her. She hoped they all looked alike to her daughter as well.

"I'm partial to the orange one," said a voice behind her.

Shelia turned and was startled to recognize the voice's owner. "Paul!"

"Hello, Shelia. Long time no see."

"Well I'm not the one who left for Europe just minutes after graduation without bothering to say good-bye."

"Ouch." Paul clasped his hands to his chest. "You really know how to hurt a guy."

Shelia blushed. "Sorry. I've been waiting 10 years to say that, and now I wish I hadn't."

"I guess I had it coming." Paul smiled. "So what's new? Do you come here often?"

"Far too often, I'm afraid," replied Shelia, shaking her head. "A few months ago my daughter won a goldfish at the PTA carnival. Unfortunately, the poor thing died two days later. Luckily, I was able to replace it before she got home from school," she confided. "She would have been heartbroken."

Paul nodded sympathetically. "Then what are you doing here today?"

"That was seven fish ago."

They shared a heartfelt laugh before Paul's expression turned serious. "You have a daughter?"

"Alyssa. She's five. Started kindergarten last fall. She's beautiful, brilliant, and destined to become anything except a marine biologist."

They laughed again before Shelia asked, "How about you? Any kids?"

"No kids, no wife, no dogs, no cats, no fish." Paul sighed. "College started right after I returned from Europe, and I've been on the run ever since. Now that I've finished my residency, I came home to set up my practice."

"You're a doctor?"

"Pediatrician."

"I'm impressed."

"It was either med school or elementary teaching, and then I got a financial aid grant, so med school it was."

Shelia laughed once again. "Well, I'm the one who became an elementary teacher."

"Now *I'm* impressed!" Paul looked deep into her eyes as he continued, "But then, I always knew you'd be great with kids—"

"Kids!" Shelia blurted out, glancing at her watch. "Today's the day Alyssa learns the facts of fish life. I've got to dash to pick her up from junior soccer practice." She waved a hand at him as she turned to leave. "Nice to see you, Paul, welcome home!"

Paul's brow wrinkled in thought as he watched her disappear. She had not been wearing a ring on her left hand...

The next afternoon, Shelia's teaching partner, Beth, asked, "So he didn't ask for your phone number or where you lived or what school you taught at or anything?"

"I didn't give him the chance to ask much," replied Shelia. "I never expected to see him again, and I certainly wasn't prepared to run into him at Mel's Hardware."

Beth sighed. "Well, honey, the fact is, he's back."

"Yes," said Shelia, "and if he wants to find me, he'll find me."

"You're forgetting," said Beth, "he probably has no idea what your last name is now."

When Shelia arrived at soccer practice that afternoon she discovered her daughter lying prone on the first row of bleacher seats. The assistant coach held an ice pack to a rather nasty-looking goose egg on Alyssa's forehead.

"I think she'll be fine," said the coach, "but you better have her checked out, just in case. She's such a little go-getter! She booted the ball so hard that she lost her balance and fell flat on her back. Another player couldn't stop in time and tumbled over her, causing a chain-reaction. In the pile-up Alyssa got kicked in the head."

Shelia was still filling out the insurance forms at the hospital admitting desk when the nurse came to take Alyssa to the examining room. "Wow, this is sure fast service," she said, following them down the hall.

The nurse nodded. "We're more able to stay on top of things since Dr. Rathburn joined our regular rotation."

"Dr. Rathburn? Paul Rathburn?"

"Yes, do you know him?"

"We, uh, we went to high school together." Shelia felt her cheeks grow warm.

Paul entered the cubicle as the nurse helped Alyssa onto the examining table. He went straight to the child and stuck out his hand. "Hello," he said, shaking her hand, "what's your name?"

"Alyssa."

"Alyssa Wilson," said Shelia from behind him. "She's my daughter."

"Shelia!" Paul's eyes lit up. "I was wondering when we'd bump into each other again, but I didn't think it would be quite this kind of bump!" He ran his thumb softly across the purple knot on Alyssa's forehead.

After peering into her eyes with his penlight and asking a few questions about school and soccer, he turned to Shelia. "No permanent damage," he proclaimed. "I'm sure her father will be happy to hear that."

"Her father lives out-of-state," replied Shelia, putting a protective arm around Alyssa.

"In that case," said Paul, writing on his prescription pad, "here's my recommendation." He tore the top sheet off the pad and handed it to Shelia.

She glanced at the note. *"Would you and Alyssa like to go out with me Saturday afternoon?"* Caught off-guard, she looked first at Paul, and then Alyssa.

Paul cleared his throat. "I thought perhaps we could do something quiet and restful while she recuperates."

"Like what?" asked Shelia.

"Like, I was thinking maybe Alyssa would enjoy visiting the aquarium."

"The aquarium?" Shelia replied, puzzled.

"You know, Mommy," said Alyssa excitedly, "the place with all the big goldfish!"

Shelia laughed. "Of course... the place with all the big goldfish." She looked again at Paul and could have sworn she felt her heart flutter. Turning back to Alyssa she said, "Well, sweetheart, if that's what the doctor ordered, then I guess we'd be silly not to follow his advice!"

A Magical, Musical Christmas

Marlene flipped through the yellow pages, vocalizing her dismay to her neighbor and best friend Shelly, as she did so. "There's no listing for music, musical instruments, musicians, pianos, piano tuners, or tuners of any kind... Oh, the joy of living in a small town!" She shook her head. "Got any suggestions?" She handed Shelly the phone book.

"As a matter of fact," said Shelly, setting down her coffee mug and accepting the proffered book, "I do."

Marlene raised an eyebrow. "Ok, Mrs. Smarty-pants, just where are you going to find a piano tuner for me?"

"I'll call the church," said Shelly matter-of-factly. "Somebody must tune all their pianos. Between the sanctuary, the fellowship room, and the choir room, they've got three of them."

A sigh of relief escaped Marlene. She smiled at Shelly. "How long were you going to let me stew about this before you offered this choice bit of information?"

Shelly smiled back. "Not too much longer. Since your Christmas party isn't for another two weeks, I still had a few days grace before I came to the rescue." She placed a call to the church office, got the needed information, and wrote the number down. "Here you go," she said, pushing the notepad in front of Marlene. "Think you can take it from here?" She stood to leave, gave her friend a hug and said, "Try not to stress so much, it's not good for you." She ducked out the door before Marlene could reply.

"You're in luck," said the elderly-sounding male voice on the other end of the line. "This is my busiest time of the year, but I think I can squeeze you in next Thursday at 4:30. Will that be okay?"

Marlene thought quickly. "Yes," she said, "that will be fine. I won't be home until 5:30 myself, but I have a neighbor who can let you in."

Thursday evening, Marlene hustled through her own front door and came to an abrupt halt. She heard a strange yet wonderful combination of music, singing, and laughter coming from her living room. She shrugged out of her coat and went straight to the source of the merriment.

Shelly was standing next to the piano, holding a child's book of popular Christmas tunes open so that she and a young curly-haired boy Marlene didn't recognize could both see the words. In a nearby rocking chair sat another unfamiliar man about Marlene's age, rocking and singing along without looking at the book. An older man stroked the piano keys with gusto and was encouraging them to sing another verse.

"Well," said Marlene, making her presence known, "this certainly looks like a Norman Rockwell moment!" She looked questioningly at her friend. "Who are all these people, and what are they doing in my house?"

Shelly laughed. She put her hand on the senior gentleman's shoulder. "This is Mr. Santano, the best piano tuner in at least three counties." She pointed to the man in the rocking chair. "And this is Mr. Santano, his son." She turned the boy to face Marcene. "And this handsome young fellow is Mr. Santano, the son of the son."

"Pleased to meet you," said the Santanos in unison, nodding their heads.

"And it took all of you to tune my piano?" asked Marcene.

"It's a family affair," said the Santano in the rocking chair. He had the same curly hair as the boy, and a warm and genuine smile like his father. "Dad doesn't drive any more, and my son comes along so we don't need to hire a babysitter."

"I'm too old for a babysitter," protested the young man. "I come along to help Grandpa do the tune-ups."

"And he's a pretty good little assistant, too," chimed in the elder Santano. He extended his hand to Marlene. "My name's Jim," he said.

"And I'm James," said his son.

"Let me guess," said Marlene, bending down to look the youngest Santano in the eye. "Is your name Jimmy?"

"Heck, no," he replied. "My name's Eddie." Then he grinned. "Well, actually, it's James Edward Santano the third."

Marlene smiled. "It's nice to meet all three of you," she said, making brief eye contact with each of them.

James stood up and cleared his throat. "I believe," he said, looking at his watch, "that we're through here, and it's Eddie's turn to make dinner."

Marlene was puzzled. She turned to Shelly with an inquiring look.

"These three guys are all bachelors," said Shelly, "so they rotate the cooking responsibilities."

"And tonight it's macaroni and cheese!" said Eddie excitedly. "I make it all by myself, too!" He fairly bounced with anticipation. "Dad taught me how to follow the directions on the box and now I'm a gourmet cook!" He gave Marlene another big grin and lowered his voice. "Only I can't remember what 'gourmet' means."

Marlene laughed. "It means 'very good' and I just bet you are."

James touched his son's shoulder. "Time to help Grandpa pack up his tools."

While Eddie did as he was told, Marlene said goodbye to Shelly, who needed to get home to fix dinner for her own family.

"And what are your plans for dinner tonight?" ask James. "I'll bet Eddie wouldn't mind making a double batch of his famous mac 'n cheese." His deep brown eyes seemed to imply much more than a simple dinner invitation.

"Say yes!" said Eddie, hopping up and down again.

"Well," said Marlene, surveying the smiling trio, "I'll say 'yes' on one condition." She hesitated while the three of them looked at her expectantly. "You must promise me you'll all come to my Christmas party next weekend and help us sing carols."

"It's a deal!" said Eddie, without waiting for his father to respond.

"It's the best deal I've heard in a long time," said James, meeting her eyes.

Jim snapped his toolbox closed and headed toward the door whistling, "It's beginning to look a lot like Christmas…"

A Fine Pair

Her friend Susan was right about one thing, thought Betty as she surveyed the classroom. There were plenty of men here. She counted 16 of them, if you included the 10 high school boys taking the community college evening class, and just four women, including Susan and herself.

"Welcome to Beginning Woodworking," said Mr. Paul, the instructor. "Since this is just a six-week introductory class, we'll need to familiarize ourselves with safety equipment right away." He held up a pair of industrial goggles.

Oh swell, thought Betty, *we get to look like scuba divers while we make fools of ourselves at the same time.*

"Cool," said one of the boys, "we'll look just like scuba divers."

Betty bit her lip to keep from laughing. She turned to Susan, who rolled her eyes.

The rest of the first class was devoted to a lecture concerning the shop safety procedures and identifying the various machines. Mr. Paul was warm and enthusiastic the entire two hours.

"Too bad Mr. Paul had a wedding ring on," said Susan as they walked to the parking lot. "He's cute."

"I didn't notice," replied Betty. "I was too busy taking notes."

"You didn't notice he was cute, or you didn't notice

he wore a wedding band?"

"Either one."

"Girlfriend," exclaimed Susan, "you're slipping!"

The second week, Mr. Paul announced that he was pairing the students up for actual time in the shop. Betty prayed she wouldn't be partnered with one of the high school students. Her prayer was answered.

"Can you believe it?" whispered Susan. "He put us together! How are we ever going to talk to any of the men if we're never going to get the opportunity to work with them?"

"Here's a thought," said Betty, glowering at her, "how 'bout we learn something about woodworking while we're here?"

Susan laughed. "Okay, okay... I knew it wasn't a dating service when I signed us up, but I didn't think you were going to take woodworking so seriously."

The fifth week Betty received a call from Susan just minutes before class time. "I don't feel so well," she told her friend. "It's just a cold, but I don't want to give it to anyone else. I know it's our turn on the lathe, but you'll have to partner up with someone else tonight. Sorry."

"I hope you feel better real soon," replied Betty. She considered just skipping the class herself, but she had already picked out her lathe project and was looking forward to working on it.

Arriving at the school, Betty busied herself with the preparations for her assignment. Tentatively, she approached Mr. Paul. "My shop partner is home with a cold," she explained. "Is there someone else I could work with tonight?"

Mr. Paul smiled at her. "You bet," he replied. "Stan Thompson's partner is out ill also. Must be the season."

Betty nodded and picked out a suitable piece of wood. She approached Stan hesitantly and said, "I hope you don't mind…"

"I don't mind at all," he said, grinning, "but I have to warn you… I'm afraid I'm an embarrassment to the male gender when it comes to woodworking." He held up his piece of wood. "I'm making a very simple candlestick, and I'm hoping that it isn't too much of a challenge for my skill level."

Betty laughed. "Me, too!"

"You're an embarrassment to the male gender too?" Stan asked playfully.

"Me, too, I'm making a candlestick!" She flicked her stick of wood in his direction.

"I saw that!" said Mr. Paul. "No horseplay in the shop area or you'll be banned for the rest of the class!"

Betty's cheeks burned hot. "Thanks a lot, Stan," she hissed under her breath.

"What did I do?" Stan whispered back. "I'm the innocent victim here. You're the one who threatened me with a semi-lethal weapon!"

"Semi-lethal weapon?"

"Well, if it was an actual candlestick already, it might actually be lethal," Stan replied. "You know, like in the game 'Clue'? A candlestick is one of the possible murder weapons."

Betty said nothing. She turned her back on him and pulled on her goggles. "Ladies first," she said, approaching the lathe.

The time passed quickly, and at the end of the class, both Stan and Betty had a reasonable facsimile of a candlestick. "This turned out really swell," she said, beaming at Stan.

"Mine, too," said Stan, rubbing some furniture polish into his completed project. He returned her smile. "But I've been thinking…"

"Uh-oh," teased Betty, "could be dangerous."

"If you'd let me finish…" He took off his safety glasses and looked at her thoughtfully. He said nothing until he was sure he had her full attention. "I've been thinking that dinner by candlelight would be a whole lot more fun if there were two candlesticks on the dining room table."

"Well," said Betty, "there's one class left. Maybe Mr. Paul will let you make another one next week."

Stan rolled his eyes. "I was thinking…" he paused, waiting to see if she was going to interrupt him again. When she remained silent, he continued, "Maybe you'd like to bring your candlestick over and have dinner with me tomorrow night."

It finally dawned on Betty that Stan was asking her for a date. "Gee," she said, "you must think I'm really dense."

"Dense, preoccupied or disinterested?"

Betty grinned. Susan had been right all along. Woodworking class was a wonderful place to meet a nice man. "None of the above," she said to Stan. "What time would you like my candlestick to be there?"

Stereotypically Yours

Leesa had read only the first three paragraphs of the short romance story before she flung the magazine clear across her living room. "Stupid stereotypes!" she shouted to no one in particular. "I hate stereotypes!"

Her cat Bubba opened one eye but did not stir from his cozy position on her lap. She stroked him absentmindedly while she continued to speak aloud. "How come all the women in those stories are no older than 25, and they all have to be so darn gorgeous?" she asked the cat. "And how come the definition of 'gorgeous' always begins with the words slim, trim, thin, petite or slender?"

Leesa, a large, well-proportioned woman in her forties, personally preferred to describe herself as having "an hourglass figure with plenty of time to spare." Divorced nearly 10 years, she knew the odds of any single woman finding true love in a small coastal town were not so good. And the odds were even worse for those women who were not deemed 'gorgeous' by society's standards.

"It's a small gene puddle we live in, Bubba," she lamented as she rose from her recliner and unceremoniously dumped the cat on the floor. "Phooey on all those men seeking anorexic women with long, flowing, chestnut hair."

Leesa laced up her tennis shoes, hopped in the car, and drove a few short miles to her favorite section of ocean beach. She did a few full-leg stretches and gauged the wind before choosing the direction for today's walk.

A quick scan of the area revealed only a handful of walkers and joggers, a couple children building sandcastles under the watchful eyes of their parents, and several teens flying kites. There were some distinct advantages to living in a small coastal town after all, and relative solitude was one of them.

Walking briskly along the edge of the ocean Leesa felt her spirit lift. She smiled; it worked every time. *Must be all those good endorphins slurping down some serotonin cocktails,* she mused.

A strong breeze whipped her short wavy hair about her face, and a half mile from the car she paused for a moment to fully zip her lightweight jacket.

"Mind if I walk along with you?" The deep male voice startled Leesa, and she involuntarily jumped at the sound of it.

"I'm sorry. I didn't mean to frighten you," continued the man. "I thought you could hear me coming up behind you. I'm the guy doing all the heavy breathing back here, huffing and puffing in an effort to keep up with the pace you've been setting." He smiled, and Leesa noticed the faint trace of dimples.

"I guess I must have been a little lost in my thoughts," she said, while quickly sizing him up for potential danger. *He looks harmless enough,* she thought. It was broad daylight, there were other people on the beach, and he didn't appear to be carrying a chain saw. She grinned. Her mother would not approve, but why not take a small chance on such a nice day?

Although Leesa usually preferred to walk alone, in his well-worn baggy-kneed gray sweat suit and dark blue stocking cap, there was something quite endearing about him, a vulnerability maybe, that tipped the balance.

"Sure," she replied with a shrug, "I guess it wouldn't hurt to have some company."

"Thanks. I'll try not to slow you down," said the man. He stuck out his hand. "The name's Eric. Eric Miller."

"I'm Leesa Wilson."

They shook hands, and quickly fell into step. The wind picked up with the changing of each tide, and any words they might have exchanged blew away before they could be spoken. Leesa was relieved; small talk was not her forté. Yet the silence was more of a companionable nature than an awkward one, and she felt comfortable walking with this man at her side.

Leesa, content with not being forced to engage in witty conversation during their walk, stole a few quick sidelong looks at this Mr. Eric Miller. Late forties, she figured, or maybe early fifties, she amended, noting the salt and pepper wisps of hair sticking out from under his cap and the crow's feet around his eyes.

Crow's feet. Leesa acknowledged the tone of negativity that resonated with that term, whereas "laugh lines" had a positive connotation. *Semantics aren't that much different from stereotypes,* she thought. She smiled to herself as she continued to appraise the man beside her.

Eric's lips were slightly parted as he pulled every breath in through his mouth. He was obviously not used to this much exertion, if and when he exercised.

When they drew even with Fisherman's Rock, now fully exposed and easily accessible during low tide, Leesa did an abrupt about-face and came to a halt. "This is as far as I usually walk before heading back," she declared.

"Thank goodness!" exclaimed a heavily-winded

Eric. "I was afraid I'd have to make the return trip in an ambulance." He leaned forward and rested his hands on his knees, fighting to catch his breath. "You walk every day?"

"Almost," replied Leesa. "I must admit I don't enjoy walking in the rain, but most of the time I do it anyway because it always makes me feel so darn noble after I force myself to brave the elements."

"I just moved here," replied Eric, "so I haven't experienced much rain yet. I hear it's legendary."

Leesa laughed. "Just imagine turning your morning shower all the way to 'cold' and walking into a 45 degree angle of freezing water for an hour."

Eric exaggeratedly shivered. "No thanks! I think cold showers are above and beyond my fitness resolution."

Together Leesa and Eric began their return trip in the same easy silence. With the wind now behind them, they were back at their vehicles in what Leesa deemed as way too short a time.

"Whew! You're a real dynamo!" panted Eric, leaning against his car, which happened to be the only other car on the approach and therefore parked right next to hers. "Or were you just trying to outrun me?"

Leesa, at a loss for words, hoped the question was rhetorical.

Eric wiped his face with the bottom of his sweatshirt, then pushed up his sleeve and glanced at his watch. Leesa followed his gaze and made a mental note that he wore no wedding ring. Which didn't mean a thing, of course, but at least it didn't dampen her interest.

"Same time tomorrow?" he asked.

"I'll be here," she replied with a smile, "unless, of course, it's raining."

Eric tipped his head back and contemplated the

brilliant blue sky and the few scattered puffy white clouds. "In the unlikely event of stormy weather," he said, "would you mind giving me your phone number? I don't want to take a chance on losing you. Not when I may have been lucky enough to stumble upon the perfect personal trainer."

Leesa dug in her fanny pack for a scrap of paper and a pen. She jotted down her number and handed it to him.

"If Bubba answers, ask him to take a message."

"Bubba?"

Leesa hesitated just long enough to observe his disappointment. "Bubba's my cat."

Eric clasped his hand to his chest and feigned a weakness in his knees. "That's twice today you've nearly given me a coronary. I hope you'll be kind enough to dial 9-1-1 the next time you scare me like that."

"Don't worry," replied Leesa, "I'm on a first-name basis with all the local paramedics."

"Is that so?"

"Yes," said Leesa, grinning broadly, "I'm a doctor."

Eric slid completely down the side of his car and collapsed on the sand in a fit of unbridled laughter.

"What's so funny about my being a doctor?" asked Leesa, her face growing hot and a tinge of irritability entering her voice. "Haven't you ever met a female doctor?"

Eric sat on the ground and continued to laugh. "I start work at the hospital next week," he finally gasped out. "I'm a registered nurse."

Leesa's surprise quickly turned to hearty laughter. When they recovered some composure, she offered Eric her hand and helped him to his feet. She was certain she could hear the unmistakable sound of a thousand stereotypes shattering like glass.

A Slam Dunk

"I hope you don't mind me saying this, but you just might be the saddest-looking clown I've ever seen."

Charlene looked up from the table where she sat trying to twist a blue balloon into some semblance of a giraffe. Looking into a pair of compassionate deep brown eyes, she was suddenly self-conscious in her curly orange wig, red nose and bright pink and purple jumpsuit. She mustered up a weak smile. "It's my first school carnival," she confessed, "and I'm having a little trouble making these balloon animals."

Robert nodded sympathetically. "I've never tried it myself. Although I once went for a hot air balloon ride, I'm afraid that's the limit of my ballooning experience. My creative talents might fall a bit short of making animal shapes from small ones."

"You never know until you try." Charlene pulled an inflated balloon from the basket in front of her. "Here. You don't even have to blow this one up."

KA-POW! Charlene laughed as Robert grimaced. "Just call me 'Robert the Inept'," he said, picking up the pieces and placing them in the trash can. She couldn't help but notice that he wore no wedding ring.

"Okay, Mr. Inept," Charlene teased, "how about you just blow one up for me and then I'll show you how to twist it around without making all the noise." She handed him a red balloon.

It took a bit of effort to get the balloon to cooperate, but Robert did as he was told and then handed it back to her. She quickly manipulated it as two young children approached the carnival booth with their mother in tow. Charlene handed the girl the red balloon dachshund.

"A wiener dog!" exclaimed the delighted child.

"I want one too!" said her brother.

Dachshunds were Charlene's specialty, and she quickly made a second one from a green balloon and handed it to the boy.

"Auntie Charlie! Auntie Charlie!" A 10-year-old girl ran up to Charlene and embraced her. When Charlene turned to introduce her niece to Robert, he had disappeared. So much for that, she thought, and shrugged it off.

"Are you having fun, honey?" she asked, noting the multi-colored butterfly painted on Kristy's right cheek.

"Yep! Sure am!" Kristy tugged on Charlene's hand. "Can you come meet my teacher?"

"Not right now, sweetie." Charlene smiled. "You talked me into helping out today, and I take my job very seriously, even if I do look a little silly. How 'bout I meet your teacher later this afternoon?"

"Okay, Auntie!" Kristy bounded away to join some friends at the dunk tank.

Charlene watched as her niece handed an event ticket over to the woman running the booth and picked up a softball. "You get two tries to dunk Mr. Pinkston," said the woman. Kristy giggled and jumped up and down with excitement.

A man dressed head to toe in a bright yellow slicker, rubber boots and Sou'wester hat climbed out on the small platform above the water. *He looks a lot like a big bathtub duck,* thought Charlene. She pitied the man; her niece had played little league for years and she had a pretty good arm on her.

Kristy wound up and let it fly. She hit the edge of the target but not the bull's eye. Undaunted, she picked up the second ball. While her friends shouted words of encouragement, she took aim, and heaved it with all her might. *KER-PLUNK!* The man splashed down into the tank and came up sputtering. The crowd clapped and cheered, and Kristy took several exaggerated bows.

Charlene grinned and gave her niece the "thumbs up" sign, then reluctantly returned her focus to creating another giraffe. The afternoon wore on, and as five o'clock approached, she was more than ready to shed her pancake make-up and clown attire.

Promptly at closing time, Kristy reappeared at her booth. "Did you see me?" she asked. "I hit the bull's eye! I dunked Mr. Pinkston!"

"Poor Mr. Pinkston." Charlene clucked her tongue and wagged her head. "Does he work here at the school?"

"Auntie! Mr. Pinkston is my teacher!"

"Kristina Anne! You dunked your teacher?!"

"She sure did," said a now-familiar voice. "And let me tell you, that water was cold!"

Charlene stopped packing up her booth to look once more into Robert's eyes. His curly brown hair hung in small wet ringlets around his face. "Oops." She laughed at his pained expression.

"I'm sorry I didn't get a chance to properly meet you earlier. Kristina reminded me at school all week that her Aunt Charlie was going to be a clown here today and I was to be sure to say hello… Luckily, I know how to swim, so I'd lived to properly introduce myself."

"Oh, Mr. Pinkston," said Kristy with a sigh, "it wasn't that deep."

"Well, then, I guess it's lucky I'm so tall."

Charlene liked his sense of humor and the easy way he bantered with her niece. "Kristy, maybe we should buy Mr. Pinkston a cup of coffee as a peace offering," she suggested. "We wouldn't want him to catch a cold or anything."

Robert grinned. "You wouldn't be just clowning around with me, would you?"

Charlene and Kristy both groaned and rolled their eyes.

"Tell you what," said Robert, "you can buy the coffee if I can buy each of you a hamburger. With all that swimming this afternoon, I really worked up an appetite."

Charlene considered, but only for a moment, making a bad pun about his swimming skills by shortening his first name to "Bob," but thought better of it. He might think her joke was all wet, and she certainly didn't want to risk not seeing him again.

"I think hamburgers would be great!" interjected Kristy. "And French fries! All those strikes I threw gave me a really big appetite too!"

Robert picked up Charlene's balloon supply basket. "After you, Madam Clown," he said as the three of them, laughing and talking like old friends, hustled out to the parking lot.

Meant to Be

Marcia couldn't believe it. Things like this happened to other people, not to her. She gingerly walked around the back of her car, careful not to slip on the frozen pavement while assessing the damage. From what she could see, the car might still be drivable. But first she'd have to get help removing it from the ditch.

She punched in the number for the auto club on her cell phone. "We should be able to get someone out there in a little over an hour," a harried voice told her. Apparently, she was not the only one having trouble in the icy driving conditions.

Marcia then dialed her boyfriend's number. *Boyfriend?* That word still didn't seem to fit her relationship with Victor. They'd been dating for several months, and he was the one who had planned this long getaway weekend for the two of them, but she still felt as if he were holding himself back.

"Where are you?" Victor asked impatiently when he answered the phone. "Our flight leaves in two hours."

"The roads were slicker than I thought," Marcia began. "I'm stuck in a ditch an hour from the airport."

Victor didn't even stop to ask if she were hurt. "You'll never make the plane," he said. "I guess you'll have to take a later flight."

"*I'll* have to take a later flight?" Marcia echoed, not

sure she'd heard right.

"Well, you don't expect me to give up hours of my vacation weekend just pacing around an airport, do you?"

"No, I guess not."

"Then I'll go on ahead, and you can call when you know how soon you'll be joining me."

Marcia reluctantly agreed and returned the cell phone to her pocket. She got back into the car and started it up so she could run the heater. Unfortunately, the only radio station she could tune in played sad country western songs, one after another.

She spent the first half hour feeling sorry for herself. She took a good look in the rearview mirror at her curly brown hair, hazel eyes and freckled nose. *He's lucky to have me,* she thought. *He's lucky I'm so understanding.* Marcia's self-pity turned to righteous indignation. *How rude of him! How inconsiderate! What a jerk!* By the time the tow truck arrived, Marcia was raving mad at the whole world.

"It's about time you showed up," she barked.

"Whoa!" said the driver, throwing up his hands in mock surrender. "I don't know what got you into such a tizzy, but you don't need to take it out on me."

"Oh my gosh," said Marcia, coming quickly to her senses. "I'm so sorry... You're absolutely right. I had no business biting your head off like that. It's just that now I've missed my flight and my...my... *friend...* went on without me, and..." her voice trailed off.

The driver removed the glove from his right hand and extended it. "The name's Kent," he said, pointing to the side of the truck where his name and phone number were clearly displayed. "Kent Richards. Now don't you worry, I'll have you out of this ditch and on your way in no time."

Marcia shook his warm hand and looked up into his

compassionate blue eyes. "Thank you," she said softly. Then she pulled her coat tightly around her and shivered as she stepped out of the way so he could get straight to work.

Kent was right. In no time at all, he had hooked up to her car and pulled it back onto the edge of the road. "Mighty slippery out here this morning," he remarked as he filled out the paperwork for the service. "You might want to drive a little slower until you get to the city limits; the roads are just fine after that."

Marcia nodded, handing him her auto club card.

"It's none of my business, uh…Marcia Tarkinson," said Kent, reading from her card, "but I've been wondering what kind of …*friend*… would just up and leave you stranded like this?"

"I've been wondering the very same thing," Marcia replied with a slight nod as she signed the service slip. "And I've been thinking that maybe I wasn't meant to make that flight. Maybe I just wasn't meant to be going much of anywhere at all today."

"In that case," Kent said with a big smile, "there's a little Mom and Pop diner about a mile from here. Could I buy you a cup of coffee to get you warmed back up?"

Before Marcia could reply, her cell phone began to ring. Glancing at the number on the display, she looked up at Kent. He raised a questioning eyebrow and she disconnected the call.

"Yes," she said, returning Kent's smile, "a cup of coffee would be great."

"I'll follow you," said Kent. "So I'll be right there if you if need me."

Marcia looked into his warm dark eyes again. *Yes,* she thought, *a man like you would always be right there for me.*

Say "Cheese"

"Brie?" asked the dark-haired woman behind the deli counter. "You would like me to recommend the best Brie?"

Harold nodded. "I'm attending a very special party this evening."

"Well, Monsieur, if you want the best Brie, then you must go to France." The way she said "Mon-sewer" and "Frr-raahnce," putting a few extra letters into the words, made Harold flinch, and left no doubt about the phoniness of her accent.

"In that case…" Harold managed a wan smile, "I'll take the second best."

"Suit yourself, *Monsieur.*"

Harold noted the playful grin she sent his way, and forgave her the accent ruse. The woman had an engaging smile and beautiful brown eyes framed by wisps of short curly hair peeking out from under her food handler's cap.

While she cut and wrapped a thick wedge of Brie from a massive cheese wheel, which looked to Harold just like all the others, he noticed she wore no wedding ring. And although no wedding ring didn't necessarily mean she wasn't spoken for, it gave him a moment's pause.

"That will be $36, Monsieur."

"Thirty-six dollars for a slice of cheese?!"

"Perhaps Monsieur wanted a smaller wedge?"

"No, no… This will be fine." He felt his face flush as he pulled a credit card from his wallet. So much for making a good impression. Now she probably thought he was cheap. Or broke.

The woman processed his card and handed him the receipt. "Have a good time at your party, Monsieur Bronson."

"You have me at a disadvantage," said Harold, wishing she would quit saying 'Monsieur' like it left a bad taste in her mouth. "You know my name from my credit card, but I don't know yours."

"Suzette. Suzette Ecru." She pointed to the name pin on her lapel.

Harold felt his face coloring for the second time in minutes, but there was something about her perpetual smile that made him determined to get to know her better. "Well, Suzette Ecru, how will you be celebrating Bastille Day?"

"I am having dinner with my sister tonight, Monsieur. She is cooking a festive meal in celebration of France's Independence."

Harold's invitation had been decorated with little French flags for just that reason. He tried to hide his disappointment.

"Perhaps another time," said Suzette, already forced to turn her attention to the next customer.

"Perhaps another time," echoed Harold. He was out in the parking lot before he realized he hadn't asked for her phone number. Well, at least he knew her name…

*   *   *

Susan Brown spent the rest of the afternoon kicking herself. Why had she let her boss, Mr. Rameau, talk her into putting Suzette Ecru on her ID tag? "It will give you an extra air of authority," he had said. Big deal. Now a really nice guy had no chance whatsoever of finding her number in the phone book.

At five minutes before six there were still last-minute customers coming into the deli. Mr. Rameau would never let her out of here while there was still money to be made. Susan sighed. Now she would be late for dinner, and her sister Ellen was somewhat of a stickler for punctuality.

Finally, at quarter to seven, Susan tossed her apron in the hamper, grabbed her coat, and headed straight for her sister's house. No time to go to home and change clothes, she would just have to borrow something from Ellen's closet.

Susan let herself in the back door, raced through the kitchen and flew up the stairs. Ellen was two steps behind her.

"Where have you been?" asked Ellen. "I was beginning to think there'd be an empty chair at the dinner table."

As Susan explained, Ellen found her a simple, yet appropriate, dark blue sleeveless dress. She tied a red and white scarf around Susan's neck and stepped back to appraise her little sister. "You look terrific." She nodded her approval. "You're really going to 'wow' our new foreign language teacher."

Susan stopped with her hand on the doorknob. "You didn't!"

"Didn't what?" asked Ellen with mock innocence.

"You didn't set me up with another one of your stodgy old teacher friends did you?"

"Ah, come on," replied Ellen, "you'll like this one."

"That's what you said about the math teacher you

set me up with last New Year's Eve, and he was so absorbed in calculating the minutes since the millennium he didn't even *think* about kissing me at midnight."

Ellen giggled. "Okay, so I was wrong about Mark. But this new guy speaks both Spanish and French, so he must know a *little* something about romance. Or did 'Mr. Right' just happen to wander into the deli today and you're holding out on me?"

"Not a chance." Susan sighed and started down the stairs. "Great job with the decorations, Sis," she said, noting the streamers forming an arch into the dining room.

"Thanks," said Ellen, "I had a lot of help." She lowered her voice, "Your dinner date showed up an hour early with enough red, white and blue crepe paper to deck out the Eiffel Tower."

"My *dinner date?*" Susan choked on the words. "Just how many people are invited here tonight?"

"You mean, all together...counting Dennis and me?" asked Ellen.

"Ellen! You told me this was a full-scale seven-course French cuisine dinner party. Now don't you go and tell me there will only be four of us!"

"Sorry, little sister..." Ellen grinned wickedly. "I didn't think you'd show up if you knew all the details."

"Right you were, and right you are!" Susan turned abruptly and headed for the stairs.

"Please don't go!" interjected a deep male voice.

Susan whirled around again and came face to face with Harold Bronson, looking more than a little disconcerted at seeing her there. He opened and closed his mouth, at a complete loss for words. Finally, he held up a bottle of French wine, turning it for her to read the label. "I promise I'm better at selecting wines than cheeses."

They stared at each other in awkward silence.

"Susan," said Ellen, trying to quickly fill the void, "I'd like you to meet Harold. Harold, this is my charming, yet horrifically outspoken little sister, Susan."

"We've met," said Harold, laugh wrinkles crinkling up the corners of his gorgeous green eyes. He gallantly extended his arm. "And will the mademoiselle do me the honor of accompanying me to dinner?"

It was Susan's turn to blush. All she could manage in reply was a softly whispered, "Oui."

Seeing is Believing

"Trust me, Roger, you'll enjoy it," Estelle pleaded with her son. "I don't want to have to think about you sitting out in the parking lot while I'm in the pool doing my physical therapy. Just try it once or twice. It will help keep you fit."

Roger hated to say no to his mother, but if he spent her therapy hour in the car working on his laptop, maybe he could keep up with his job responsibilities. When his mom had hip surgery, Roger had willingly volunteered to drive her to and from the pool three mornings a week. But now, a little more than two months later, he felt a bit guilty taking so much time off.

"Your work will wait, Roger," said Estelle as though reading his mind. All you do is work, work, work." She smiled a motherly smile. "Now if it were a social life you were missing out on to take your poor old mother to her exercise class, I'd insist you let me ride the bus—but work can wait."

Roger shook his head. His mother often remarked, none too subtly, how she'd undoubtedly be too old and decrepit to play with any grandchildren that might come along if he didn't get busy and find himself a nice woman to marry. But first Roger had insisted he was too busy with college, and then he was focused on beginning his career. Now... Well, now he really didn't have any excuse. Mom's

temporary disability was certainly not standing in his way.
"Did you hear me?" continued Estelle. "I said, 'next week the pool is having a special where guests may attend for free.' Why don't you plan to come with me just three times? Three measly times. Is that so much for a mother to ask?"

Laughter erupted from both of them. Estelle did not play the "Poor Me" part very well at all. "Okay, okay." Roger gave in. "But if any of those little old ladies start hitting on me, I'm out of there!"

"Deal." Estelle enthusiastically bobbed her head, her blue eyes sparkling. "And don't worry, dear, if you can't keep up with the arthritis and therapy exercises, you can always do them half speed. The instructor doesn't mind a bit."

The following Monday Roger emerged from the men's dressing room and tentatively approached the pool. "Over here!" Estelle called, waving her arms exaggeratedly. "Over here!" She was already standing waist deep in the shallow end, doing a series of warm-up stretches while holding on to the side of the pool.

Rock and roll music blared from the speakers of a portable CD player, and for a moment Roger forgot that he was doing this to please his mother. This might be fun.

The hour passed quickly, and at one point Roger wondered if one could actually work up a sweat while exercising in a pool. The instructor had taken them through quite a workout, mobilizing every muscle group in turn. He felt surprisingly invigorated as he waited for Estelle to join him in the car.

"Sorry I took so long to change, honey," she said as she eased herself into the seat and strapped the belt across her lap. She smiled broadly. "Julie had a lot of questions about you."

"Julie?" asked Roger as he started the car and began backing out of one of the many handicapped spaces near the door.

"Julie. The instructor. She's just a few years younger than you, and she's single, by the way."

"Mother, please…." Roger drew out the word 'please' like it had three or four syllables. "Don't tell me this whole thing was a set-up!"

"Don't 'Mother' me, young man! And don't try to tell me you didn't notice how cute she is, either!"

Roger laughed. "Sorry to spoil your little scheme, Mother, but how could I notice *anything* about her? I wasn't wearing my glasses in the pool. For all I know, she's got warts on her nose from years of working around all that chlorine! Thanks, but no thanks!"

Estelle's brow furrowed and her mouth dropped open. She sighed. "I forgot about your glasses," she admitted.

She sat in silence as Roger skillfully maneuvered the car toward the exit. "Anywhere you need to stop before I get you home?" he asked her.

"Well, I do need a couple things at the grocery store. Shouldn't take but a few minutes."

"No problem," replied Roger, grateful for a change of subject. A short time later he was heading into the store clutching his mother's quickly scrawled shopping list in his hand. It was considerably longer than the "couple things" she had originally said she needed, but he didn't mind. "Sit tight," he told her, giving her an affectionate peck on the cheek. "I'll be back in a flash."

But by the time he emerged, Estelle had her car window rolled down and was deep in an animated conversation with an attractive young woman. Roger took a good look at the woman as he placed several bags of groceries into the trunk of the car. *Now there's a woman I wouldn't mind meeting,* he thought to himself.

He slammed down the trunk lid and returned the cart to the store. The women had their heads together and were laughing heartily about something as he approached.

"Roger, look who's here!" Estelle cheerily called out.

"Hi," said Roger, walking around to the passenger side of the car. "I'm Estelle's son Roger."

"I know," said the woman. Roger was struck dumb by the incredible green eyes scrutinizing him. She stuck out her hand. "I'm Julie."

"Julie?" Roger stammered. "Julie from the pool?" When she nodded, Roger continued, "I, uh, I didn't recognize you with your clothes on. Um, I mean, you look different when you're not wearing your swimsuit. Uh, I meant to say—"

Estelle and Julie laughed again as Roger turned a startling shade of scarlet.

"Your mother has invited me to dinner," said Julie, playfully batting her eyelashes. "She said you'd be there too. What would you like me to wear so that you'll have no trouble recognizing me?"

Roger regained enough of his composure to flirt back. "You can wear anything you like, just so long as you wear that terrific smile to go with it."

"Deal," said Julie, rewarding him with another beautiful grin.

"Deal," echoed Estelle, winking at Julie, "and I'll make sure Roger wears his glasses."

Roger said nothing. He could clearly see for himself that his mother just might be on to something.

White Horses

Della considered herself a realist—a woman of the new millennium. She knew better than to be so naïve as to still believe in romance. Yet there was something that compelled her to keep looking for that knight in shining armor, the man she was certain would ride into her life on a white horse. Surely there must be one such remaining chivalrous savior, and Della had vowed to find him.

Picking up the newspaper one Saturday afternoon, she skimmed the personals ads, a habit she hadn't been able to shake even after years of disappointment. No Prince Charming listed again this week, so she flipped to the grocery ads and reached for her shopping list. A new market had recently opened a little less than a mile from her apartment. If she bought only the barest of essentials, so she wouldn't have too much to carry home, she could get in a little exercise by walking to and from the store.

"Grand Opening, Saturday 9 to 5. Free hotdogs, pop, balloons! Special appearances by local TV personalities! Bring the kids to see the Teenage Mutant Ninja Turtles! Many more surprises!

Great, thought Della, *now I'll have to wade through a million screaming children trying to get an autograph from a pizza-eating cartoon character.* Sighing, she put on a light jacket, grabbed her purse, and headed for the door.

Della's mood improved considerably during her

walk. A sunny autumn day, the wind was whirling leaves down the sidewalk ahead of her. She shivered, and pulled her windbreaker tightly around her. The sun was deceiving—it was much colder than it looked—but she was invigorated, nevertheless.

After wandering up and down each aisle of the new supermarket, Della found herself standing in front of a rack of romance novels. Swell. She hadn't read one of these since she was in her early twenties. She had too much to do this afternoon, she argued with herself, and yet she seemed drawn to the book covers sporting blissful-looking couples with moony expressions on their faces.

A green rubber-gloved hand reached around her and plucked a book from the rack. "Here," said the deep-voiced owner of the hand, "I recommend this one."

Della turned to see the person behind the voice, and was startled to be suddenly face-to-face with one of the Grand Opening Celebrities, although she could not be sure just which Ninja Turtle he might be. Recovering quickly, she glanced down at the book he offered. "Magic in the Stars," by Francine Neumann.

"Ever read anything by this author?" the turtle asked her.

"No," she said, finally finding her voice. "Have you?"

"Every single one."

"I didn't know turtles read paperback novels."

"You probably don't think we're the least bit romantic, either, do you?"

Although Della couldn't be certain, she sensed he was smiling behind that big green mask. "Are you?"

"Well, I'm supposed to be out front signing autographs for the kids and posing for pictures, but instead

I followed you in here hoping for a chance to talk with you," he said all in a rush. "Do you consider that romantic?"

"I– I'm not sure," said Della, puzzled. *Was this guy hitting on her?*

"Let me get right to the point then," the turtle continued. "Would you like to have coffee with me?"

Delia was taken aback. "I'm flattered," she said, a little harsher than necessary, "but I make it a policy to avoid getting picked up by aggressive reptiles in the grocery store." With that, she turned and walked briskly to the checkout counter.

After paying for her groceries, Della was dismayed to discover that the sky had turned dark and rain was falling in torrents. She hesitated under the eaves, noting that the "local TV personalities" had all disappeared with the bright October sun.

"Second chance for that cup of coffee…" The voice was familiar, but when Della turned this time, she found herself staring into the deepest blue eyes she had ever seen. "Frank. Frank Newman." He extended his hand and Della shifted her groceries in order to shake it.

"Della Smithson."

"Well, Della," said Frank, "can I at least give you a lift somewhere?"

"I… I… We got off to a rather bad start, didn't we?" Della began. "I'm sorry I was so rude in there."

"I understand. I should have realized you might be turned off by my costume, but I just didn't want to let you get away." He was still holding her hand.

"So, uh, how long have you been a turtle? I mean, do you make a good living doing supermarket openings?" Della was already stacking him up against the number one item on her list of minimum criteria: "Employed."

Frank laughed. "It pays the rent. Romance writing isn't all that lucrative until you get well-established."

"Romance writing?"

"My pen name is Francine Neumann." He saw her confused look and continued. "Women buy more romance novels when they think the book was written by a female."

"Oh, now I get it." Della smiled. "So, how much did you make on the book I just bought?"

"Enough for coffee. How about it?" His eyes held her gaze, and Della knew instinctively that in this century a green rubber suit just might be able to pass for a suit of shining armor.

"Where's your car?"

"Right over there," he gestured. "It's the one on the end."

Della couldn't stop laughing as they splashed through the puddles on the way across the new parking lot and settled into his white mustang convertible. She wondered if he had a dog named Prince.

A Fable for Modern Times

Once upon a time, in the far away city of Gnol Hcaeb, which, as everyone knows, is the slightly backward Soviet sister city of Long Beach, Washington, an enterprising young woman, whom we shall call Rhoberta, went into business for herself.

In the United States Rhoberta would have been hailed as a woman ahead of her time, an opportunist, an entrepreneur, or at the very least, a shrewd businesswoman. In Russia she was simply called "The Shrew."

Rhoberta had saved her rubles for years and years, and had decided that her sojourn into the predominately male-oriented business world would be through the tavern door. She opened her bar, called "The Office," on the corner of 3rd and Main, capitalizing on the idea that the name alone provided a suitable alibi for her illustrious clientele.

Hooray for capitalism! Her bar was an immediate success, and she was overwhelmed by the amount of bulsevism that flowed through her tavern doors each evening. She was surrounded nightly by beer-guzzling, pretzel-chomping, back-slapping men. A virtual supermarket paradise for a single woman such as herself, yet even this pseudo "heaven on earth" did not satisfy Rhoberta.

Rhoberta soon grew lonely for her own kind. Were

there not other independent, self-assured women who were interested in a night out now and then? She took a hint from the American sister city and instituted a "Ladies Night" at the tavern. But very few women showed their faces inside her establishment, free beer nuts notwithstanding.

On Thursdays Rhoberta was losing money—something she was not fond of. Surely there must be some drawing card to bring out the women of the Soviet Union. The men, of course, could be entertained by playing pool, darts, pull-tabs, and watching almost any sport on the big-screen TV that involved wagering their entire paycheck. Women, however, didn't seem to take to boxing, or cockfighting, although being a liberated woman, the latter did, however subtly, appeal to Rhoberta's own inner sense of word play.

Again she turned west—to the city of Long Beach. What was it that brought out the women of that fair town to the more prestigious libation stations of the area? And it was then that Rhoberta learned that Chippendales was not only a brand of furniture.

Being on a rather stringent budget, Rhoberta decided to move cautiously into the area of entertainment. She interviewed several likely candidates, and settled on an unemployed magician named Noglac as Gnol Hcaeb's first male bubble dancer. Magicians at that time were a kopek a dozen in the Soviet Union, and Rhoberta had no trouble convincing him that he would be playing to much larger audiences at her place of business. Noglac readily accepted the offer.

Now instead of sawing ladies in half, he made them swoon and sway. Instead of making rabbits disappear, he made his clothes vanish in a haze of beer suds. He became an overnight success!

Rhoberta's business grew rapidly, with "Ladies' Night" becoming the hit of the whole Ukraine. Every Thursday it was standing room only. There was only one small hitch in Rhoberta's otherwise triumphant life. She had fallen head over heels in love with her undulating prestidigitator. Her carefree single days were indeed numbered.

Readers may think that love would be a good thing for our heroine, settling her down, making her less anxious—but alas! Not so for Rhoberta! Imagine, if you will, giving your heart to a man who, every Thursday night promptly at 9 p.m., would be shirking his habiliments in front of 200 screaming women.

And every Thursday night, rain or shine, Rhoberta had to suffer watching the object of her affection frolicking in the suds to the thunderous chanting of "Noglac! Noglac! Ekat em yawa!" which, for those readers who are way ahead in this story, obviously translates to the American "Calgon! Calgon! Take me away!" And these women meant it, each and every one of them.

While Rhoberta thoroughly enjoyed watching the rubles roll in, she was certainly not fond of watching these women ogle her man, beer suds or no beer suds. To alleviate her heartache, Rhoberta saw only two ways out. Either she had to find another 200 gorgeous, single, dancing Russian stud-muffins for the private entertainment of these women of Gnol Hcaeb, or she must turn her back on her fellow countrywomen and quietly pack up her oxcart and move on, preferably under the cover of darkness.

*   *   *

Rhoberta really likes living in America, and is currently traveling the talk show circuit promoting her highly successful book, "Praises and Pitfalls of Female Entrepreneurship in the U.S.S.R."

Calgon, who immediately Americanized his name, has found his niche as the rising star of prime-time laundry commercials, promising Rhoberta, after "love, honor and obey," that the only thing he will make disappear in the suds are the dastardly stains of chocolate, grass, and red wine.

Rhoberta has assured him that if he finds he cannot stick to this commitment, he can add blood to the stains he'll need to have removed. Make no doubt about it, she is, after all, a very clever, very shrewd woman, who plans on living happily ever after.

Pure Poetry

Edie sat quietly at her display table, watching the happy, boisterous crowd around her at the bazaar. This fundraiser for the Barking Lot Animal Shelter was a great idea. There were hordes of people snapping up the donated cakes and cookies and playing all the silly carnival games.

Her booth, however, was not attracting much interest.

"Hello," said a man suddenly standing in front of her.

"Oh! Hello!" Edie replied with a start. "I'm sorry, I didn't see you."

The man smiled. "That's ok," he said, nodding. "You see me now."

I sure do, thought Edie, feeling her cheeks growing warm. *My goodness, what a handsome man.* She returned his smile as he reached down and picked up one of the small poetry chapbooks from the table.

"D-do you l-like to read p-poetry?" she managed to stammer.

The man was skimming through the book's table of contents. "I'm afraid I don't know much about it," he admitted. "I just know what I like when I read it."

Edie quickly regained some of her usual composure. "That particular chapbook is a collection about animals," she began. "Dogs and cats, mostly, but there are a few about ferrets, hamsters, horses, parrots, and even one about a pet goat. The book was written especially to raise money for the Barking Lot."

When the man did not respond, Edie stopped her nervous chattering. She knew it was best to keep quiet while a potential customer looked through the books. She waited patiently while he read a few of the poems. She noted his curly hair, his broad shoulders, and the fact that he wore no wedding ring.

The man smiled again when he looked up from his reading and caught her staring at him. He grinned. His eyes were a beautiful shade of brown, reminding her of warm milk chocolate. And when he smiled, the crinkles at the corners of his eyes made them fairly dance.

"These poems are very good," he said. "I like them very much. Did you write any of them yourself?"

Suddenly self-conscious, Edie just nodded.

"Which ones?" the man persisted.

"All of them." Her voice came out uncharacteristically soft.

"Really?!"

"Yes." Edie nodded again.

"That's outstanding! I've never met a real live poet before."

Edie's face flushed for the second time. "I've always loved the way words sound, and the way you can string them together to form vivid pictures."

"Well, *you* sure can, anyway. Me, I've never been able to write anything nearly as nice as you do." He set the book back down on the table and looked closely at her with a steady gaze. Then he held out his hand. "I'm John. John Harper."

Edie shook his hand. "Edie Meyers."

"Nice to meet you, Miss Meyers… It is Miss, isn't it?" he asked hopefully.

"Yes, it's Miss," said Edie as she reluctantly pulled her hand away.

John exhaled a sigh of relief. "Good! Now you won't think I'm out of line for asking you if you'd like to have lunch with me."

"Lunch?" Edie could barely squeak it out. "Now?"

"Yes, lunch," said John, looking at his watch. "They do let you take a break to eat, don't they?"

"I'm the only one manning this table, " replied Edie.

"You could put up a little sign saying you'd be back soon," said John hopefully.

Edie shook her head. "I'd hate to miss a single sale. I'm donating 100% of the proceeds to the shelter, and every little bit helps provide for the homeless animals."

"Hhhmmm…" John contemplated this information. Finally he asked, "Then what time does the bazaar end?"

"Not until 4 o'clock." Edie sighed. "And that's a little late for lunch, I'm afraid."

John thought for just a second before he spoke. "And… what if you sell out?"

Edie burst into a heartfelt laugh. "From your mouth to God's ears!"

"No, really, it could happen." John reached down, put his hand over hers and whispered. "Do you solemnly promise to have lunch with me if you sell out?"

"Of course I will!" Edie laughed again. "It would be pretty silly to be sitting here without any books to sell, wouldn't it?"

"In that case," said John, reaching for his wallet, "I'll take all of them."

"John! You can't be serious."

"It's for a good cause," continued John. "And as a bonus, I get to have lunch with a real live poet. So you see, it's a win-win situation."

It certainly is, thought Edie as she picked up her pen and began autographing the small pile of chapbooks. *It certainly is.*

Falling for Him

Jenna Tyler stood with hands on hips, surveying her apartment. "It's definitely missing something," she finally admitted to her best friend, Alice.

"I've been trying to tell you the very same thing the entire four months you've been living here," said Alice. "It's time we visited that garden center on the next block."

"The garden center?" echoed Jenna. "Whatever for?"

"You need something that's living and growing and will green up the place."

"You mean like a plant?"

"Exactly!" Alice beamed. "I know you're not allowed to have pets here, but at least you could have a few plants to tend to."

Jenna hesitantly followed Alice out the door, down the elevator, and around the block to "Smitty's Nursery."

A nice-looking man about their age approached them. "Hi," he said, extending his hand. "I'm Hal Smith, but you can call me Smitty."

Jenna felt a tingle go clear through her when they shook hands.

The women explained their mission, and Smitty helped them select a few low-maintenance houseplants.

"What about this?" asked Alice, holding up a beautiful blooming fuchsia basket. "You could hang it from the railing on your balcony."

"I don't know." Jenna furrowed her brow. "There might be some kind of rule about hanging baskets out there."

Smitty laughed. "Don't worry, there's no restriction on flower pots or baskets on the balconies where you live."

Jenna felt the hair on the back of her neck stand up. "And just how do you know where I live?" she asked suspiciously.

Smitty's face turned bright red. "I'm sorry. I should have mentioned it before—we live in the same apartment building and I've seen you around."

Jenna said nothing, but she quickly took her selections to the cashier, paid, and then she and Alice hurriedly left.

"He was really cute," Alice said as they toted the plants back to Jenna's place.

Jenna shook her head. "That was too weird. I don't remember ever seeing him in the elevator or laundry room."

"Maybe it's because you've always got your nose pressed into a book."

"You're right." Jenna laughed. "Ok, so if I do happen to see him again, I'll try to be a little friendlier."

Alice nodded. "Men as cute as that don't just fall from the sky, you know." She set the box of plants she'd been carrying down on Jenna's kitchen counter. "And I'm glad you decided to get that fuchsia basket. It's gorgeous."

Jenna walked out on her balcony with the plant and the women tried to figure out how to attach it to the railing. Finally Jenna got a wire coat hanger and together they twisted it around the metal handrail.

Alice stepped back to survey their work. "I think

that'll do it," she said. She looked at her watch. "And I've got just enough time to get home and put the roast in the oven." She paused. "Are you sure you won't join us?"

"No, thanks," said Jenna. "I'm right in the middle of a good mystery novel, and I want to finish it this evening."

"I rest my case," said Alice, laughing. "You'll never meet any nice guys if you don't get out more." She gave her friend a hug and headed for the door. "Tootle-loo!" she called out, closing the door behind her.

"Tootle-loo," said Jenna softly, picking up her paperback. She flipped it open to her bookmark and settled in on the couch to read.

KABAM! A thunderous crash jolted Jenna from the couch a short while later. She ran out onto the balcony and discovered her hanging basket had disappeared from the railing.

Peering over the edge, she saw what was left of the basket lying on the sidewalk. Potting soil and blooms littered the pathway, and Smitty stood there looking up at her.

"It's alright!" he called out. "It missed me!"

"Oh my gosh!" said a horrified Jenna. "It could have killed you!" She didn't wait for the elevator, but quickly bolted down the three flights of stairs.

Smitty was gathering up what was left of her plant when she got there. "I'm so sorry!" she exclaimed, bending to help him pick up the pieces. "I guess using a coat hanger was a bad idea."

Smitty laughed. "Maybe not..." he said slowly. "Maybe now you'll think you have to make it up to me by agreeing to join me for dinner."

"Dinner?" said Jenna.

"Yes, dinner," replied Smitty. "And then, after you

decide I'm not such a bad guy, maybe next weekend you'll invite me over to show you how to attach a proper plant hanger to that railing."

Jenna smiled. "Dinner sounds great," she said, "but I'm buying. It's the least I can do for nearly dropping a plant on your head."

Smitty returned her smile. "Jenna," he said, "you've got yourself a deal."

Behind the Scenes

Jeanie tried to scoot lower in her seat, but the community theater volunteer coordinator had already spotted her, and was making a beeline.

"There you are!" Marlene gushed as she approached. "I've been saving a spot for you next weekend."

"Next weekend?" Jeanie furrowed her brow, confused.

"How about Saturday night?" asked Marlene, consulting her clipboard. "Will you be available to take tickets for that performance?"

Jeanie breathed a sigh of relief. "Yes, of course I can do that." She nodded and smiled sheepishly. "I'd forgotten I'd signed up to volunteer, but it's okay, I'm not doing anything at all next weekend."

Marlene scribbled Jeanie's name down on the list. She tapped her pencil on the paper a few times, then said, "I haven't gotten anyone to volunteer to push cookies and pour punch during intermission, so I might need you for that, too, if you don't mind."

"Sure thing," said Jeanie. She wondered if her social calendar would ever have anything more on it than attending playhouse board meetings and volunteering during theater performances.

Saturday evening Jeanie took a little extra time with

her hair and makeup. She wanted to look her volunteer best. She showed up at the theater a few minutes early to learn how to run the box office.

Marlene was bubbly, almost giddy, as she told Jeanie she'd found absolutely the most "perfect person" to man the cookie sales. "But I definitely need you to be there, too!" she finished adamantly.

Dutifully, Jeanie showed up at the refreshment table as soon as the lights came up for intermission. She quickly set out boxes of cookies, napkins, and cups, then looked around for Marlene's idea of the "perfect person."

A man about her age was carefully carrying out the punchbowl from the kitchen. It was full to the rim, and Jeanie watched as he gently set it on the table before her.

"Whew!" he said, smiling and stepping back. "I think Aunt Marlene was just testing my nerves of steel by filling it so full."

Jeanie smiled back. "Marlene is your aunt?"

"Yes," said the young man. "Marlene is my very pushy but adorable aunt, who wouldn't take no for an answer. She insisted I come here tonight to volunteer, even when I told her I had other plans this evening."

There was no time for further conversation as the hungry throng of theater patrons surrounded the refreshment table. Jeanie hardly had a moment to steal a glance in his direction as he served the punch. He was cute, with curly hair and warm brown eyes, but he'd also made it clear he'd had other plans before agreeing to come to his aunt's aid.

In no time at all, the lobby lights blinked twice to signal the start of the second act. Without a word, her fellow volunteer carried the almost-empty punchbowl back through the kitchen door.

Marlene bustled up as Jeanie was putting the few remaining cookies into a box. "Well, what do you think?" she said happily.

"What do I think about what?" asked Jeanie.

"About my nephew, of course! Isn't he just perfect?"

The light suddenly dawned, and Jeanie didn't know whether to be flattered or insulted. "Marlene! You were setting us up!"

"Yes, of course I was," said Marlene, matter-of-factly. "When you said your weekend was free, I took the liberty–"

"But he's not available," interrupted Jeanie. "He said he had plans for tonight before you insisted he come help out."

"Oh pshaw!" said Marlene, shaking her head. "He was only going to watch football with some buddies of his. I'm sure he's not seeing anybody."

"Oh I'm not, huh?" Marlene's nephew spoke from right behind them.

Jeanie's cheeks were red-hot as she turned around. The man was looking at her with an amused expression. He put out his hand. "My name's Matt. We got so busy there, I didn't have time to properly introduce myself."

"Jeanie," she said, timidly shaking his hand.

"Well, I'll leave you two alone then," said Marlene, bobbing her head up and down and quickly heading for the backstage area.

Matt laughed good-naturedly. "Aunt Marlene means well."

"Yes, I—I'm sure she does," said Jeanie quietly.

"So..." began Matt. "Have you seen this play before?"

"Several times."

170

"Then you wouldn't mind missing the second half to have a cup of coffee with me at the diner next door?"

Jeanie smiled. "I'd like that very much."

As she went to retrieve her coat, Jeanie thought Marlene might have been on to something when she'd told her she'd found the most "perfect person" to man the cookie table.

Matt might turn out to be the most perfect person for her, too.

A Genuine Nice Guy

Betty looked authentically horrified after I told her my plans for the day.

"You can't be serious!" she exclaimed, pressing her palms against her cheeks in an expression of alarm.

"Oh, yes, I'm very serious," I told her. "I'm tired of sitting at home waiting for some nice gentleman to ring my doorbell. It's time to give fate a little push."

Betty shook her head and clucked her tongue. "Flora Abbott! I knew all that time you spend on your computer could only lead to no good."

My dear friend Betty is hopelessly stuck in the past century.

"Here's what he looks like," I told her, handing over a picture I'd printed out. "And I've included everything I know about him—name, date of birth, address, model of car he drives, and so forth."

"You really think he's been telling you the truth about everything?"

"I'll find out today when I meet him."

"But what if he's an axe murderer? What if I never hear from you again?"

Betty was still wringing her hands when I got into my car to drive the short distance to the city park. I'd agreed to meet this man—Thomas Knudsen—only after weeks of computer chats and a few conversations on the phone.

I was happy to see the park full of people. I parked the car and quickly checked my hair and makeup in the visor mirror. I got out of the car and easily blended in with families and friends enjoying the nice summer day. I kept an eye on the bench where Thomas and I had agreed to meet.

Promptly at 10 o'clock, a tall, pleasant-looking, gray-haired man carrying a pink carnation approached the bench and sat down. He looked around expectantly. Even from a distance I could tell he was nervous. Good. So was I.

Gathering my courage, I walked up to him. "You look just like your picture, Thomas," I said, extending my hand.

Thomas stood up and shook my hand. He handed me the carnation. "But you look even prettier than your picture," he said, smiling. He motioned to the park bench and we both sat down. An awkward silence settled in.

Finally, Thomas cleared his throat. "Flora," he began, "to tell you the truth, I was afraid one of us might chicken out." He chuckled. "I was also afraid it might be me."

"I would have really hated that," I said softly.

"Well… uh…" Thomas cleared his throat again. "So you said you like baseball. Have you been to any games this year?"

"No, unfortunately, I haven't been to the ballpark at all this season." I looked down at my hands in my lap. "And to be quite honest, it isn't much fun to go to the games alone—there's no one to share my garlic fries with!"

"Then maybe we can go together sometime." Thomas paused. "I mean, once you get to know me better."

I nodded, considering. "I think I might like that."

"Going to a ballgame, or getting to know me

better?" he teased.

"Both." I grinned, finally beginning to relax a little.

"Then why don't we start with lunch? There's a Mexican restaurant just a block from here. I think I remember you writing me that you liked Mexican food."

"Lunch is a very good place to start," I said, standing. "And your memory is very good. You remembered both that I like baseball and what I like to eat."

"Do I get brownie points for that?" asked Thomas, also standing.

"No brownie points," I replied. "Just this." I reached into my right-hand pocket and produced a loaded squirt gun. I playfully shot water at him.

"Hey! Hey now!" Laughing, Thomas put up both his hands to fend off the assault of sprinkles. "What's this all about?"

I laughed too. "A girl can't be too careful," I explained. "And I didn't know whether you'd turn out to be a nice guy or a creep. The nice guy gets the squirt gun."

Thomas furrowed his brow and tilted his head, peering at me quizzically. "So... If the nice guy gets the squirt gun, then just what does the creep get?"

I took his proffered arm for our short walk to the restaurant, already certain that this would be the first of many meals together. I leaned closer to him and whispered, "In my other pocket is pepper spray."

"Pepper spray!" Thomas looked shocked.

"Don't worry," I said, "I only brought it along because my friend Betty insisted. She'll be very relieved I didn't have to use it."

"So am I!" said Thomas, squeezing my arm and laughing again. "So am I!

No Missed Connections

"This can't be happening!" Marci said aloud. She was alone at the airport, but surrounded by hundreds of people trying to make their way home for the Thanksgiving holiday.

On the digital display board above her head, the word "Delayed" flashed annoyingly after the name of her destination and flight number.

"Looks like we're both going to be here a little longer than we planned," said a deep male voice close behind her.

Marci turned, and her shoulder travel bag connected with the midsection of a man holding a brief case in his left hand, a coffee cup in his right hand, and a thick newspaper folded and tucked under his right arm.

"Oh! Excuse me!" she gushed, her face turning red.

"Totally my fault!" The man shook when he laughed, and Marci was glad his coffee cup had a lid on it. "I was standing so close because I didn't have a free hand to put my glasses on!"

Marci nodded. "I can certainly relate." She motioned to her wheeled carryon with the handle protruding, parked in front of her. Over the top of it draped her sweater. "I'm only going to be gone for a few days, so I'm travelling light, but it's still a lot to juggle."

The man smiled and introduced himself. "I'm Steve

Adamson."

"And I'm Marci Thomas." She extended her right hand and they both started laughing again. "We'll just pretend we shook hands," she said.

"How very understanding of you." Steve smiled and tilted his head. "Do you live here in this town?"

Marci nodded. "I moved in with my aunt a couple years ago when she needed some help after hip surgery." She smiled, and continued, "I found out I liked caregiving so much that now I'm taking classes to be a nurse."

"Wow," said Steve, "I'm impressed."

Marci's face flushed again. "Is this your hometown too?"

"It is indeed," said Steve, "but I do a little travelling for business."

"You're not going on a business trip over Thanksgiving weekend?"

"I volunteered," replied Steve. "The married guys all wanted to be home with their families."

"Now I'm impressed," said Marci. "How very generous and thoughtful of you!"

A short silence fell between them, but Marci did not feel at all uncomfortable. They'd only known each other for a few minutes, but she was totally at ease with him.

"No telling how long we'll be waiting," said Steve. "Shall we find a place to sit where we can continue our conversation?"

Marci nodded. "I'd like that."

A little over three hours passed like minutes, and Marci was actually sorry when their flight number was called.

Steve's company had provided him with a First Class ticket. He went to the counter and tried to upgrade

Marci's seat to First Class as well, so they could sit together, but the flight was totally sold out.

"It's okay," she said with a shrug. "But it was awfully nice of you to try."

"I'll catch up with you at the other end," said Steve as they boarded. "I promise."

Marci knew he meant what he said. They'd developed quite a connection in the airport, and her heart skipped a beat as she thought of the possibility of them dating after they both returned from their holiday weekend.

She squeezed into her center seat in coach, and settled down to read a nursing magazine. She didn't want to think any more about Steve sitting there in First Class, just 25 or 30 feet away.

Marci became so engrossed in an article she barely noticed when the pilot turned off the seatbelt light. "You are free to move about the cabin," he said.

"Excuse me," said a familiar deep male voice to the man sitting on the aisle beside Marci, "but would you mind sitting in First Class for the rest of the flight?"

"You gotta be kiddin' me mister," said Marci's neighbor. "What's the catch?"

"The catch," said Steve, winking at Marci, "is sitting right next to you, and I don't want to spend the whole flight away from her."

The woman sitting on the other side of Marci gently elbowed her. "Oh, that's so romantic!"

Marci turned scarlet.

"I hope you don't mind," said Steve, buckling his seatbelt. "There was no one like you to talk to up there."

"There was no one like you to talk to back here, either," Marci admitted shyly.

They chatted amicably until the plane encountered

some turbulence on their descent. Steve grasped her hand. "I hope you don't mind this, either," he said. "I get a little nervous when the air gets bumpy."

Marci smiled and looked out the window. Her mother would be waiting in the airport, and Marci just knew she'd be thrilled to have another guest for Thanksgiving dinner!

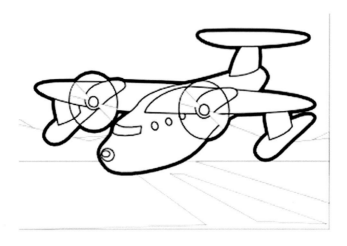

A Heartwarming Evening

On one of the coldest afternoons of the year, a car skidded off the icy road and into the utility pole right in front of my house. Fortunately, the driver, an elderly woman, wasn't hurt, but she sure was shaken up.

"Please come inside," I told her as I helped her from the car. "Is there someone we can call?"

She nodded. "My son. My son will know what to do."

Inside the house, the power had gone out. "Did I do that?" asked the woman.

"No, you didn't hit that pole nearly hard enough." I flicked on the flashlight I keep on the hall table. "Good thing my phone works without electricity."

"Oh dear, oh dear," she mumbled, wringing her hands as she sat on a chair in the kitchen. "I'm afraid my son is going to be terribly mad at me."

"Mad?" I echoed. "I'll bet he'll be thrilled that you're alright."

The woman shook her head. "My son Charlie works for the Public Utility District," she said with a mother's pride. Then she sighed. "And now it's all my fault he won't be able to take Betsy to the movies tonight."

I patted her hand. "Let's take this one step at a time." I handed her the phone and left the room in search of candles while she made the call.

Returning, I noticed my new friend was in much better spirits. "Charlie is on his way," she said. "And you were right; he's more relieved than upset." She mustered up a smile. "I'm Ethel, by the way."

"Nice to meet you, Ethel. I'm Suzanne." I placed several lighted candles on the table in front of her. "Do you know anything about tropical aquariums, Ethel?"

She chuckled. "I'm afraid not, dear. Why do you ask?"

I sat down next to her. "I'm worried about my fish. I don't know how long they'll last when the tank water cools."

"Oh my!" said Ethel. "I certainly hope the power won't be out that long."

The PUD truck arrived just moments later. Charlie bounded up the porch steps, and I opened the door to Ethel's very handsome, and very worried, son. "Mother!" he exclaimed, "Are you really okay?"

Ethel assured him she was fine, and Charlie helped her to his truck. "We'll get send a tow truck for her car in the morning," he called out.

I waved good-bye from the doorway and then began wrapping blankets around the fish tank. I didn't really think it would help, but it couldn't hurt.

Several hours passed and still no power. Night had fallen when I saw headlights approaching and a vehicle turning into my driveway. I pulled my coat around me and stepped out onto the porch.

Charlie was just getting out of his truck. "Suzanne?" he called out.

"Yes? May I help you, Charlie?"

"I'm afraid your power's going to be out all night," he said. "And my mother told me about your tropical fish."

Charlie came up the walk toting a portable generator and several extension cords. He set them all on the porch. "This will give you enough electricity to keep the little guys from freezing." He smiled. "And there might even be enough extra power for you to fix me a cup of coffee so I can warm up before I have to get back to work."

I opened and closed my mouth several times.

Charlie threw back his head and laughed. "You know, you look just like a tropical fish yourself when you do that!"

"But I... I mean... Well, I didn't think..." I struggled to find the right words. Finally I blurted out, "But what about your movie date with Betsy?"

Charlie laughed again, a full-bodied melodious laugh. "Betsy's my 10-year-old daughter," he said, while he set up the generator. "She's lived with Mom and me ever since the divorce. My ex-wife never got used to me being on-call, but Betsy knows work has to come first."

"She sounds like a very mature child," I said, holding the flashlight while Charlie ran an extension cord inside. Soon I heard the familiar hum of the fish tank.

"After Mom told her how nice you'd been, Betsy absolutely insisted I come right over to save your fish." Charlie cleared his throat and looked away. "I think one or both of them might be trying to play matchmaker."

It was my turn to laugh. "A guy who listens to his mother and his daughter might be a good guy to get to know." I started for the other room. "And now, if you'll kindly run another extension cord into the kitchen, I'd love to make us both some coffee."

"You betcha!" said Charlie, beaming. "One coffeemaker power source, coming right up!"

A Dog-gone Good Volunteer

"Hot dogs, chili dogs, Polish dogs!" Charlene called out.

She was working at the Humane Society's booth at the Kite Festival, trying to attract hungry customers from the throngs walking by. It was mid-afternoon, and business was predictably slow.

"Buy a dog, save a dog!"

That usually got people's attention, and even if they didn't buy anything to eat, many of them were happy to donate to the cause.

"You're really enjoying this, aren't you?" asked a smiling man about her age as he stuffed the donation jar with several bills.

Since he used his left hand to put the money into the jar, Charlene couldn't help but notice he wore no wedding ring.

She gave him a big, genuine smile. "Our little furry friends need us to speak up for them," she replied. "And I've got a voice that carries."

"So I noticed," said the man, laughing with her while he obviously checked out her left hand. "So I noticed."

Further conversation was interrupted by a young customer pushing his way to the counter and asking for a chili dog.

"Well, gotta go," said the man. "I'm anxious to watch the fighter kite competitions."

"Thanks for supporting our animal shelter," said Charlene, turning to dish up the youngster's order. "When you get hungry, you know where we are."

For the next two hours, Charlene was busy serving hotdogs and kicking herself that she hadn't asked the man's name, or given him her own. She hoped she'd see him again, but her shift was almost over for the day.

When Betty came to relieve her, there'd been no sight of "Mr. Handsome Kite Watcher," and Charlene almost reluctantly turned over her post. As she handed Betty her apron, she told her about the close encounter and near miss.

"So if he comes back asking about me, remember I have dibs," she told her friend.

"No promises!" Betty laughed. "If he's as good-looking as you say, I might just have to practicing batting my own eyes at him!"

Charlene tossed the dishtowel at her. "I signed up for first shift tomorrow. Just tuck all my messages in the till."

But late the next morning, the only message Charlene found was to remember to chop more onions before the lunch crowd arrived.

Eagerly, Charlene watched the passersby. "Hot dogs, chili dogs, Polish dogs!"

Noon approached, and the booth was suddenly swamped with customers. It was all she could do to roll more hot dogs around on the grill before each tray's refill was completely cleaned out. It was great to be selling so many items, but she had to move so fast, she felt like she ought to have roller skates on.

"Can I help you out in here?" The side flap of the booth tent was pulled back and Mr. Handsome Kite Watcher stuck his head in. "You look like you could use another pair of hands."

Gratefully, Charlene handed him an apron and together they managed to get a multitude of orders out quickly and efficiently.

When at last there was a little break in the action, Charlene pulled off her food-handlers gloves and stuck out her hand. "Charlene," she said. "Thanks for saving me. I was getting a little frantic."

"I could tell." The man laughed, pulling his own gloves off. "The name's Tom."

Just shaking his hand sent little butterflies racing through Charlene. She didn't want to let go, but she knew she couldn't just stand there like a schoolgirl experiencing her first crush. She released his hand and busied herself refilling the ice barrel with sodas.

"I came back last night, but you were gone," said Tom, adding buns to the warming tray. "I thought if you hadn't already filled up on hotdogs, then maybe we could go out to someplace nice and have dinner."

Charlene laughed, and the fluttering in her chest threatened to keep her from speaking. "Is the offer still good today?"

"I dunno," said Tom, grinning widely, "Those chili dogs look mighty good."

"You're in luck!" she replied. "I happen to like chili dogs. When my replacement shows up, would you like to take some and go out to watch the kites some more?"

Tom's eyes met Charlene's. "Buy a dog, save a dog?"

"It's for a very good cause."

"And I know I'd be in very good company," said

Tom.

Betty arrived a few minutes later. "Who's this?" she asked Charlene.

"This is Tom," Charlene replied. "A dog-gone good volunteer." She scooped up a generous serving of chili and poured it over two steaming hotdogs.

Tom had already taken off his apron. He handed it to Betty, and together he and Charlene walked arm in arm to enjoy their early chili dog dinner while watching the kites dance across the sky.

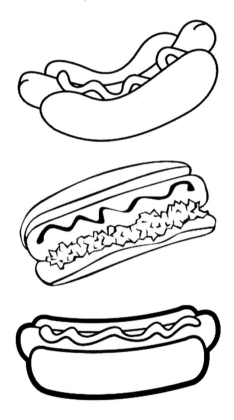

Skinny Decaf Mocha Latte

A good memory comes in handy in my work as a coffee barista. Often, I know exactly what a person is going to order after just their second time in my shop.

There's usually a line of thirsty caffeine-seekers during the morning hours, and they aren't there for chatty conversation. They just want to get their coffee and go. My memory often helps me get a jump on the orders almost before the cashier rings them up.

"Skinny decaf mocha latte," said a new customer one Monday morning. I knew he was new to the shop because I'm certain I've never made a skinny decaf mocha latte with whipped cream and sprinkles before.

The man paid for his drink, and moved down to the other end of the counter to retrieve it. He had curly brown hair and a very attractive mustache and goatee. He smiled pleasantly when I handed him his drink.

"I suppose you want to know why I put whipped cream on a nonfat latte," he began.

"I just fix 'em the way they're ordered," I replied, smiling back. I lowered my voice to whisper, "And I try not to judge."

He laughed heartily at my remark, displaying the deepest dimples I'd seen in decades. I hoped to continue our conversation, but he just thanked me for his coffee and slipped out the side exit without further comment.

Just as well, I sighed. The line for coffee extended clear out the front door.

I'd nearly forgotten "Mr. Dimples" by Wednesday, when once again I heard an order conclude "with extra whipped cream and chocolate sprinkles."

But also once again, the number of customers coming in prevented us from more than the cursory "Thank you" and "You're welcome."

I shouldn't complain. My little coffee house, a remodeled little bungalow, is tucked right smack dab into the middle of a residential neighborhood. My banker warned me against opening here, telling me that anyone wanting coffee in this area could make it at home.

Success came as a happy surprise. And at the rate it's going, I'll be paying off my loan many, many months ahead of schedule.

Thursday and Friday I kept an eye out, but my new customer did not reappear. How disappointed I felt! But on Monday he came in a little later than before, and there was time for more than a quick exchange of pleasantries.

As he took his drink from me, he told me he worked at home, just around the corner. "I'm a writer," he explained. "So I pretty much set my own hours. Today I'm getting a late start at the keyboard, but Izzy wouldn't let me work until I'd come for our coffee."

"Oh," I said, trying not to sound disappointed, "then you'd best get back before she comes looking."

Mr. Dimples laughed. "We wouldn't want that to happen." He lifted his drink in salute and went on his way.

When he came in on Tuesday, we were packed again, and I was glad I wouldn't have to make any more polite conversation with him. The cute ones, the smart ones, seemed like everyone my age, was already taken.

Wednesday and Thursday passed without a coffee visit and I must admit I was kind of relieved. But Friday, when he came through the line during the early rush, he waved my business card at me.

"Picked this up on the front counter," he said. "I'll call you this afternoon." And before I could reply, he scooted out the side door.

Call me? Although he wore no wedding ring, he'd been clear there was someone special at home—someone with whom he shared his morning coffee.

Now, I'm not one to sit by the phone—usually—but this time I found myself drawing out my closing chores longer than normal, refilling the containers with sugar packets and creamer almost an hour after quitting time.

The phone rang at 5:45. "Hello?" I said tentatively.

"Hello, Arlene!" said the now-familiar voice. "Where would you like to go for dinner?"

"Dinner? With whom?"

"Oh, of course," he continued, "I should start by introducing myself. This is David, better known as 'skinny decaf mocha latte.'"

"I know *who* it is," I said, coolly. "I just wanted to know if Izzy would be coming to dinner with us."

I could imagine his dimples as he belly-laughed. "I don't think she can make it," he finally choked out.

I said nothing.

"Izzy is my cat," he went on. "I get the extra whipped cream and sprinkles for her. She loves it."

"Oh..." I began, "I thought..."

"Do you like Chinese food?" David interrupted. "I can pick you up in 15 minutes."

"Fifteen minutes will be great," I decided quickly. "And tell Izzy I said 'Hi'."

ABOUT THE AUTHOR

Long Beach, Washington, author Jan Bono calls herself "a sucker for romance." She delights in playing matchmaker for her friends, and regularly enjoys attending "chick flicks" at her local theater. For decades, she has been writing short romance stories for submission to various national publications. Jan has written numerous one-act plays and has published several short story collections.

See more of Jan's work at: www.JanBonoBooks.com